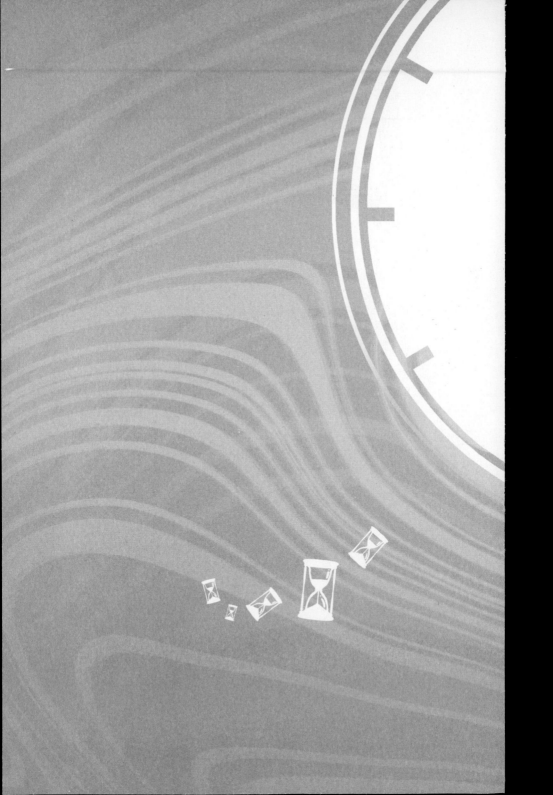

Throwback

Peter Lerangis

HARPER
An Imprint of HarperCollinsPublishers

ISBN 978-0-06-240638-5

Typography by Andrea Vandergrift

19 20 21 22 23   CPIG   10 9 8 7 6 5 4 3 2 1

❖

First Edition

For Bobby.
—P.L.

NOW

1

When Corey Fletcher was five, he saw a woman on the C train take out her teeth and argue with them. At age seven, he ran out of his house on West Ninety-Fifth Street in New York City and nearly collided with a man walking a pig.

Corey was thirteen now, and already in his life he'd seen a naked wedding by the Hudson River, an elephant lumbering up Amsterdam Avenue, an actor falling off a Broadway stage onto a trombone player, and a singing group that burped entire tunes in harmony.

Corey didn't seek out strange things. They just came to him.

But nothing was stranger than the vision he'd once observed at age seven, outside his window. It disturbed him so much he told no one, not even his grandfather, who lived with Corey's family.

And he told his grandfather *everything.*

People said Corey had an active imagination, but Corey didn't think so. He didn't imagine any more or less than other people. He just kept his eyes open. And he had a good eye. He knew this because way back when he told his grandfather about the woman and her teeth, the old man said, "Corey, you have an Ed Gooey."

It took Corey only a few seconds to realize that the letters of "Ed Gooey" spelled out "good eye." His grandfather liked anagrams. He could mix the letters of words in his head and make up new words on the spot.

"Both eyes are good, Papou," Corey replied proudly, which cracked the old man up.

"Bravo, *paithi mou!*"

Papou is Greek for "grandfather." Which sounds a lot nicer than his real name, Konstantino Vlechos, which no one could pronounce. Or Gus Fletcher, his American name. Or Odd Gus, which is what some people called him. He was a New Yorker through and through, but he liked to use Greek expressions like *paithi mou,* which means "my child." And *bravo,* which means "yay."

Of course, Corey loved his mom, dad, and sometimes

even his sister, Zenobia. But if you asked him in secret, he'd say he loved Papou best. Odd Gus—I mean, Papou— liked crossword puzzles, word games, and the New York Mets, in that order. But he *loved* hearing Corey's stories.

Well, he *did* love them, before he disappeared one year ago.

Which brings us to the story that Corey never told.

One night when Corey was seven, Papou was reading aloud from *A Wrinkle in Time*. His voice always put Corey to sleep, even when the book was amazing.

Corey's eyes were half-shut when he saw a shadow outside his window. Behind Papou's shoulder.

The Fletchers lived in a sunken, ground-floor apartment in a four-story building. So they were used to people passing by the front windows. Not so much the back, where Corey's bedroom was.

In the soft drone of Papou's voice, Corey was seeing tesseracts dancing in his head. He knew those weren't real, so he didn't think the shadow was real either.

Even when it leaned forward and pressed its nose to the glass.

It was someone Corey had never seen, someone much older than he was. But he knew who it was. He recognized the face.

It was his own.

He did not scream, although he wanted to. Instead, he lay in bed silently for hours and finally fell asleep. Papou hadn't seemed to notice. Which meant, Corey thought, that the whole thing might not have really happened. So he never said a word about it to anyone.

If he had, this whole story might have been different.

Or maybe not.

Corey, like everyone said, had an active imagination.

ONE YEAR AGO

2

On the last day Corey saw his grandfather, the old man paid a late-night visit. He chose not to wake the boy. Corey looked like an angel in his sleep. His feet already stuck out from the end of the bed at age twelve. Papou smiled sadly. Twelve years of foot growth and laughter and pizza and hide-and-seek and crazy discussions. Twelve years that his dear wife, Maria, had never known.

He gritted his teeth. He couldn't think about her now.

Over the years he'd pummeled his grief into a lump buried deep in his heart. He'd trained himself not to think about that sunny September day in 2001, when a jet plane that sounded like the end of the world stole those years from Maria.

And now he was about to lose Corey too.

As Papou carefully wrote a note, the pen dropped from his hand and clattered to the bedroom floor. He was tired, but his grandson was tireder, if there was such a word. The noise didn't wake Corey. Not a bit.

His face etched with sadness, Papou watched the boy as he mumbled in his sleep—garbled words mostly, but Papou could make out one clear sentence: "Is that you, Oliver?"

Oliver?

It had been a couple of years since they'd played Oliver and Buster Squires, Gentlemen of the Distant Past from the Town of Twit. They would crack each other up so much that Corey's mom would scold them both. By now, Papou thought Corey had grown out of that game.

Not a chance.

Papou leaned close. "Indeed, Buster," he whispered, "but we must have a good night's sleep, in order to retain the quality of our sweet body odor."

Corey smiled and let out a giggle. As his lips settled downward, he began to snore. Papou ran his fingers lightly through his grandson's dense thicket of hair. During the daylight it danced with every shade from amber to chocolate, but in the darkness it was jet-black. He knew that his grandson hated that hair now, but Corey would grow to love it someday.

Papou did not like thinking about someday. Only today. And today, his time had come.

People said time stopped for no man. It was an arrow. It marched on. It would always tell. But that was nonsense. None of those things was true.

Papou had learned this the hard way.

He kneeled and picked up the pen he'd dropped. His fingers weren't what they used to be. Before long he wouldn't be able to write at all. Placing the pen back on Corey's desk, he glanced at the note he'd written:

Dear Corey,
You look so peaceful, I don't want to wake you. Sorry, but I was called away to Canada—an emergency with one of my close friends from college. I may stay for a while. So sorry I couldn't say a proper farewell. I left you something to remember me by.

Wear it every day. Think of me. And time will fly.

XOXOX,
Papou

He carefully folded the letter and placed it into a big padded envelope he'd brought into the room, wedging it next to his genuine Civil War–era belt, which Corey had always admired. The one with the brass buffalo-head buckle stamped Oct 31, 1862.

Leaning over his grandson, he brushed the boy's forehead with a kiss. "*S'agapo, paithi mou,*" he whispered. *I love you, my child.*

He could neither stay anymore nor say any more. If he had to face Corey and tell him directly, if he had to see the look on the boy's face, it would crush him. Leaving silently was already too painful. He backed away through the door, so as not to let the boy's sweet face from his sight until the last possible moment.

Shutting the door behind him, he quietly left.

Corey turned in his sleep toward the window. In the dim city light, a small tear glistened on his forehead, from where it had dropped.

By morning the tear would be gone.

And so would the man who had left it.

THE PRESENT

3

As Corey stepped outside on a foggy Halloween morning, he was not surprised to find a horse, a buggy, and a plastic pack full of blood.

For a week, his whole block had been transformed into a set for the movie *Victorian Zombies of Olde Manhattan*. The street really did look olde. Gas lamps were installed at the curbs, plastic cobblestones were laid over the blacktop road, and all the neighbors had had to move their cars out of sight. Last night Corey had snuck a peek out his window at a noisy shoot-out scene with horses, carriages, and people in old-timey costumes. Lots of fake blood had sprayed from the actors as they pretended to drop dead. It was beyond awesome.

Now Corey knew how they did the spurting-blood

part—square plastic packs of red goo! Genius.

He strode to the blood pack, which was lying on the sidewalk. Without any traffic on the block, he could hear his own footsteps. He smelled horse manure. The whole scene made him feel like a kid in the late 1800s. Standing straight, he called out over his shoulder to Zenobia, who was climbing up the steps from their apartment, hunched over her phone: "What a glorious morning, dear sister—but, hark, what lies on yonder pavement? It suggests blood, in color and in thickness!"

"Ew," Zenobia grunted. "One of the stunt people must have dropped it. And stop pretending you're in the past. It's so nerdy. They didn't talk like that, anyway."

"How dost thou knoweth this?" Corey looked up and down the block and smiled. "Admit it, this whole thing—this movie set—it's awesome! Doesn't it change you inside? Make you feel like you've stepped into another time?"

"Pssht," Zenobia replied, which was her way of saying no, when no wasn't strong enough. "I auditioned to be an extra. But they took Emma Gruber from Number Thirty-six instead. She even got her SAG card. She's fakey, and so is this set."

"And a SAG card is . . . ?" Corey asked.

Zenobia rolled her eyes. "It means you're a professional movie actor."

"I sag. Can I get one?" Corey was thirteen and barely one hundred pounds. If you counted his stupendous nest of hair (thanks to his Greek American dad and Puerto Rican mom), he was already more than six feet tall. So in truth, he *was* in the habit of sagging when he talked to his shorter friends.

But Zenobia would not dignify his question, so he bent over to pick up the blood pack from a pile of swirling red and yellow leaves. Next to the dropped pack were a dropped fake cigarette, a dropped New York City MetroCard, and a dropped silver-chain necklace with a large oval-shaped locket, all of which (except the cigarette) he slipped into his pocket while Zenobia was looking at her phone.

Corey held up the fake-blood packet, which was labeled Property of Gotham Cinema Solutions. "How do you think it works—do they just squeeze it and . . . *goosh?*"

Zenobia sighed with great drama. For days she had been composing a symphony based on her epic poem, The *WestSidiad*, mostly during her subway rides to

Stuyvesant High School. With her red cat-eye glasses, close-cropped hair, and black-on-black wardrobe, she never seemed exactly cheery, but interruptions by Corey made her downright mad. "Well, duh, the actors can't be squeezing those things by themselves on camera, right? So the packs must be hooked up to some kind of wireless detonator. When the shot rings out, someone presses a button on a device, and—"

"*Goosh!*" Corey exclaimed.

"You said that already," Zenobia snapped. "Work on your vocabulary."

"Splursh?" Corey offered.

Zenobia groaned. "Did the hospital switch my real brother with you at birth?"

"Ha ha. Not funny."

"I'm serious. You don't look like Mom or Dad."

"I look exactly like Papou," Corey said. Which was true. "Plus, he liked to pretend to be in the past. Remember our alter egos?"

"Otto and Bimbo Something?"

"Oliver and Buster Squires, Gentlemen of the Distant Past from the Town of Twit."

"Right. He made you wear a monocle." Zenobia smiled faintly. "That was back before you became Nerd on a Stick. When you were cute. And he was alive."

"I'm still cute," Corey said. "And he's still alive."

"Corey, let's not start this again."

"Well, that's what I believe," Corey said defiantly.

"Welcome to the Never-Ending Fantasy World of Corey Fletcher." Zenobia turned silently and began walking up the street toward the subway. Corey saw only the back of her head, but he could tell she was sneering.

That was when he had his first really bad idea of the day.

He examined the blood pack. It seemed pretty clean. He spat on it, rubbed it on his shirt for good measure, then put it in his mouth. Tucking it into his left cheek, he followed Zenobia up the street. "Hey, Zenobe! Hit me. Seriously, just slap me in the face. Lightly."

She pulled out one of her earbuds and said over her shoulder, "First, that thing was on the sidewalk, so you probably have a communicable disease. Second, if you think you're going to bite down and spray me with fake blood, save it for your middle school friends. And, oh, by the way, your school is in the opposite direction."

Corey felt himself sag again. He stopped, watching her walk toward Central Park West. Then, in a perfect imitation of Papou's Greek-accented voice, he said, "Don't take any wooden neeckels!"

Zenobia ignored him.

Traffic whizzed by in both directions on Central Park West, but police barricades blocked the end of Ninety-Fifth Street, so none of the vehicles could turn in to the movie set. As Zenobia veered left toward the subway stop, Corey could hear the soft clopping of a horse behind him.

He turned.

A couple of trainers were leading a horse with a lustrous brown coat and tufts of white ankle hair up the block. They had come from the direction of the trailers parked around the corner, and they were giving the horse exercise, brushing it gently. With no cars parked at the curb, the hoof steps echoed crisply against the fronts of the four-story brownstone apartment buildings. Corey smiled. In the morning sun, the buildings glowed and the windows cast deep shadows. Columns, flat fronts, massive stoops or none, brick walls or stone—they were like people shoulder to shoulder, with different faces and personalities. Even though he saw them every day, Corey had never really noticed how unusual and unalike they were.

His phone chimed, breaking the spell. This would be Leila Sharp, his best friend, who always texted at this time. Fishing out the phone, he quickly answered.

> meet at my house 2 walk 2 school?

>> u mean like we do EVERY SINGLE MORNING lol???

> hahaha. b nice.

>> nice is my middle name. corey nice fletcher.

> don't b late. ;)

Leila liked to be early for everything. But George Washington Carver Middle School didn't start for another fifteen minutes and it was only on the next block, which meant maybe a four-minute walk.

So Corey had time. And when he had time, his mind kicked into gear.

At the moment, his mind was feeling guilty about snatching the MetroCard and the locket from the street.

Whoever dropped them would be missing them. So with his extra time he could return the items. The movie people probably had some kind of Lost and Found. And those people were always in big white trailers parked along Central Park West, which was on the way to school. He thought about returning the blood pack, too. But he decided to keep it where it was, parked inside his cheek. No one wanted a drool-covered blood delivery device.

Walking up the street, he pulled the chain from his pocket. The locket caught, so he had to give it a good yank. It was pretty big and clunky, at least an inch around, and as it popped out, the hasp sprang open.

Corey was not surprised to see a funky old faded photo inside. But he was surprised by a flash of darkness all around him—a silent, momentary blackness. Like a sudden eclipse, or a spell of blindness as if something had hit him in the head.

He let out a squeak that would have been embarrassing if anyone had been there to hear him. With his free hand he felt the top of his head. No ache, no bump, no unusual object on the ground.

Bending his knees, he took a deep breath. Then he glanced upward into a stormy sky, thick and white with fog.

It was nothing. His stomach felt a little funny, but that would be nerves. Nerves and an overactive imagination.

He glanced at the open locket in his hand, which showed a badly faded sepia photograph of a woman. She was looking off to the left, but that's about all Corey could tell. The image was so old and washed-out, she could have been a dolphin with hair.

Lightning flashed, followed by a clap of thunder. In a nanosecond, his mom would be shouting from the window for him to take an umbrella. Corey hated umbrellas.

But as he ran toward Central Park West, his hand began to sting. Now the locket was smoking hot. A tiny wisp of smoke rose from the metal.

With a muffled cry, he moved it from hand to hand until it cooled. If there was lightning, that meant electricity in the air—and maybe it had conducted through the locket. Like the key on Ben Franklin's kite. Was that possible? Could a person holding a lightning-struck locket survive?

"What the heck?" he murmured.

Leila would know. She knew everything. Forget about returning this thing. He'd take it straight to her. This was too weird to let go of.

As he tried to snap the locket shut again, he caught a glimpse of the faded portrait. Now he could make out a smile. The woman didn't seem so dolphin-like anymore. Her eyebrows were thick and her cheek was adorned with a dark mole. Her hair bunched up unevenly where it was pulled back by a ribbon.

With his free hand, he rubbed his eyes. Now he was able to see the ridge of her nose and the lace on her collar. The face was becoming clearer, the background whiter.

"Hello! You there!"

A booming voice made him nearly drop the chain. He looked up. A man with a handlebar mustache and a thick woolen uniform was riding a horse toward him. It was a different horse from the one he'd just seen, thicker chested and not nearly as shiny. The other horse and its handlers were gone, and this guy did not look happy.

Corey knew that expression. He'd seen one of the movie people with that same look the day before. It usually meant they were about to film a scene and they wanted everyone out of sight.

"Shhorry, you're shooting, right?" Corey said, his voice thick with the blood pack that was still in his mouth.

"Well, not yet, unless I have a reason to." It was an odd thing to say, and the guy gave an odd chuckle. "Say, perhaps you can help us."

"Help you?" Corey's heart sped up with anticipation. He thought about what had happened to Emma Gruber from number 36. SAG card, potential stardom! "Sure! I—I've had shhhome on-camera experiensh!" he blurted. "Once I washh in the audience of *Shhaturday Night Live*. I can do accentsh and stuff. I go to George Washington Carver Middle School, but the adminishtration gave Emma permission to be in the film. You know, that'ssh the girl you hired yeshterday? Shho they'll be cool with me doing it, too. Will I get a Shhhag card?"

The guy stared blankly. "All I want you to do is answer a few questions, big fella." He pulled a sheet of paper from his jacket, unfolding it as he showed it to Corey. It was a pencil portrait of a young guy with a wispy beard, an evil grin, and beady eyes. Printed over the portrait were the words WANTED FOR THE CRIME OF DESERTION, and under it the name FREDERICK RUGGLES. "Do you know the whereabouts of this young man?"

Corey grinned as it dawned on him what was happening—an *audition*. He wished he hadn't had the pack in his mouth, but spitting it out would look too weird. "Ohhhh, duh, of coursssh!" he replied. "Shh-horry."

"Haw! Well then, aren't you one peculiar boy!" The guy cocked his head and gave a muffled laugh. He was good. He was a professional and was not going to break character. That's just what actors did. "You know, son, you will get quite a substantial reward for information leading to a capture. How does . . . *two dollars* sound to you?"

"Gadzooksh, 'tissh a fortune, I thinks!" Corey said, furrowing his brow as he examined the old portrait. "But, land shakesh and dagnabbit, shir, I have never sheen this man in my life!"

The guy nodded. "Hmmm . . ."

Was anyone shooting video of this? Corey snuck a look around for signs of any crew. But all he saw was one man halfway up the block, with raggedy pants hiked up over his waist.

He was walking a goat.

Corey blinked hard. It wasn't the goat that caught his eye. The guy was in front of number 36, Emma's address. In the place where the apartment building had always stood was . . . nothing. Just a battered wooden fence strung together with wire and what looked like a small shack with a dirt yard.

"Sorry . . . shhorry, going off character now," Corey said, tucking the blood pack as far back into his mouth as he could. "What happened to that house?"

The man, who had begun to turn his horse around, stopped. "Excuse me?"

"Emma Gruber? She lives there. She's in the movie. This doesn't make sense. Did you guys knock down a building overnight?"

"Young man, I'm afraid very little of what you've said makes sense to me," the man replied, his face tight with concern. "By the by, may I ask where your parents are?"

This was a dream. It had to be a dream.

Corey began pinching himself. It hurt, a lot. He was not waking up. And nothing was changing.

Now the guy was dismounting, walking toward Corey. "Are you all right, young man? Shall I take you to your mama and papa? Do your mama and papa know you are outside? Do you know your address?"

He was talking to Corey as if he were four years old. Or as if he were just plain loony tunes.

Maybe he *was* loony tunes.

Corey backpedaled. He nearly tripped over a metal pole sticking up from the sidewalk. A brick sidewalk.

"Those are bricks, not cement," Corey said. "They're supposed to be cement. And that's a hitching post."

"Yes, it is," the guy said in a soothing voice. "Of course it is. . . ." He was coming closer, reaching behind him for something Corey couldn't see.

Corey looked down into the little patio just below the stairs that led to his apartment door. The windows revealed a living room with rocking chairs and a wooden table—none of which he had ever seen before. "Wait—that's my house. I was just in there. Where's all our stuff?"

The man was holding a cord now, a leather strap. With a sudden lunge, he raised his arms and reached behind Corey with the cord. He pulled it tight, pinning Corey's arms to his side. "There's a good boy. . . ."

"Hey!" Corey cried out.

"Just stay put," the man said through gritted teeth. "This is for your own safety. A little trip to the sheriff."

Corey could smell the tobacco on the man's putrid breath. He struggled to move his arms, but the guy was already tying a knot.

So he shifted the blood pack from the back of his mouth to his teeth and bit down, hard.

A gush of red goop splattered into the man's face. He cried out, staggering backward.

Corey turned on his heels and started to run. The half-tied knot quickly loosened, and the cord fell. Above him, someone let out a yell and threw a bucket of slop from a fourth-floor window that splashed to the curb and doused his ankles.

At the sight of Central Park West, Corey's knees buckled. The high-rise at the end of the block was gone, replaced by a small brick building. On Central Park West itself, a horse-drawn trolley passed from right to left.

Corey kept his balance and ran. Thunder blasted again, with a sound so loud it seemed to shake the buildings themselves. The burning sensation in his hand grew sharper and he almost dropped the locket.

"*Leiiiilaaaaaaa!*" he screamed, sprinting as fast as he could.

4

On a day like this, Corey was jealous of Leila Sharp. Ever since her dad left her family, she had been seeing a shrink once a week. He did not envy the dad part, only the shrink part. He wished he were seeing one, too. "I think I'm losing it," he said, pacing back and forth in front of her building on Central Park West.

"Stop moving," Leila said, dabbing Corey's face and shirt with wet wipes. "I think biting the blood pack traumatized you."

"You didn't hear any thunder?" Corey asked. "Or horses?"

"Just a second." Leila pulled back, scrutinizing his face. She had soft greenish-blue eyes in a field of freckles as red as her hair. She had a way of being annoying but also making Corey feel calmer. "There. All clean. Nope, no thunder. No horses. But no biggie either, okay? You have a very active imagination, that's all."

"I hate when people say that," Corey snapped. "Everyone tells me that."

"Dude, how long have I known you? You've always been this way. You're just being Corey."

"It was as real as you are, Leila! Everything changed. This guy on a horse tried to tie me up. Emma's house was gone. A man was walking a goat. Somebody threw a pail of pee out the window. This locket got super hot, and I could see every detail of the face of the lady inside. Look at her now!"

Corey held out his hand and snapped open the locket. The lady's face was nothing more than two vague eyes in a faded oval outline.

"Okay, you *do* need a shrink." Leila checked her watch. "I'm seeing mine tomorrow. But I can call her after school and before the Halloween party, and I'll tell her you're looking."

"There's a Halloween party tonight?" Corey asked, snapping the locket shut.

"Sorry for the confusion, Mr. Time Traveler, but

today is still October thirty-first, and you told me you'd be my date. So to refresh your memory, we are going to school without costumes because costumes have been forbidden this year. Then you're coming to my house for pizza after school and we're going to the Halloween party together, in costume. That last part is nonnegotiable." Leila picked up her backpack from the sidewalk and hooked it over her shoulders. "Now let's go or we'll be late."

"It's not a date," Corey grumbled. "Parties aren't *dates*."

But Leila had already started off.

With a weary sigh, Corey followed. He felt numb. He liked the idea of going to a psychologist, but it seemed weird. His family didn't do stuff like that. None of them needed to. They were too normal.

Still. What happened this morning was not normal.

They turned right onto Ninety-Fourth Street, in the direction of George Washington Carver Middle School. Leila was walking at her usual warp speed. But after what had just happened, Corey was wary. He eyed the block carefully. No horses. No weird weather. Just like every morning, yellow buses were double-parked in front of school. Just like every morning, angry drivers were stuck behind them, bumper-to-bumper. Corey had never in his life been so happy to hear the honking of twenty-first-century car horns. He quickened his pace and caught up with Leila at the base of the school steps.

A zombie, holding a severed human arm, greeted him and Leila at the front door. "Shake," he said.

Corey nearly hurled his breakfast but Leila burst out laughing. It took him a moment to realize the zombie was Mr. Skiptunis, the assistant principal. Just behind him in the lobby, a group of kids from Ms. Lee's history class were shooting questions at Wonder Woman . . . who looked suspiciously like Ms. Lee. Marching in and out of the school office were two overweight Batmen, a five-foot-two Supergirl, a not-so-Incredible Hulk, and a King Kong who was bossing people around in a muffled version of the principal's voice.

"I thought we weren't supposed to wear costumes to school," Corey said to Zombie Skiptunis. "You told us to wear normal clothes today."

"Those were *yooour* rules, not *oooours*, bwah-ha-ha-ha-ha-ha," said the assistant principal with a ridiculous evil laugh. "Surprise!"

"They tricked us," Leila said, pulling Corey through the door.

"Halloween for teachers only is a very lame idea," Corey said.

"Is that why you came to school as Grumpy?" Leila asked.

Inside, teachers in costume were acting like kids, and kids were screaming and posing for selfies. But the strangest thing was a team of people with professional-looking cameras roaming around, recording it all. Leila let out a joyous squeal. Instantly a guy with a thick beard and man bun darted over with a mic, followed by a woman carrying a big camera that said NY-2 Local News. "So, kids, what do you think of NYC Pop-up Halloween?" the guy said in a voice that was one part too loud and three parts too jolly.

"Wait, *what?*" Corey said.

The guy chuckled. "It's a thing. All over the city this year. But this is the first time a group of teachers have done it! Are you surprised?"

"It's awesome!" Leila cried.

As they asked her a few more questions, Corey slunk away. He quickly pulled out his phone and searched for NYC Pop-up Halloween. Instantly he saw images of all kinds of costumed people walking the streets of Manhattan. A guy dressed as Thor on the East Side. A team of pirates called the ARGHHH Society in the West

Village, complete with parrots on their shoulders. A snake charmer floating down Broadway on a realistic-looking flying carpet.

His mind was flying with thoughts. *A guy with a big mustache and a horse . . . a goat farmer . . .*

"Ohhhhh . . . !" Corey felt like a fool. This morning's ridiculousness all made some kind of crazy sense now. He put away the phone and smacked himself in the head. "I am such a dummy."

"I could have told you that," said Leila. She was walking toward him, away from the wandering TV team.

"No, I mean about all my weirdness this morning." Corey held up his phone. "Sorry. All that stuff I was freaking about—it must have been one of those pop-up things. Some of them are really elaborate. Right now, somebody's probably posting a YouTube clip of me spitting fake blood on that guy."

"So you're not out of your mind after all," Leila said.

"Nope," Corey replied. "Well, not completely. But maybe I'm *close* to not-out-of-my-mindness. There were still some things I can't explain."

Leila raised an eyebrow. "Like, missing buildings? Thunder that never happened?"

Corey nodded. "So yeah, maybe you should call your shrink for me."

"Just stay sane enough to go to the party tonight," Leila replied.

As they shared a fist bump, the bell echoed through the hall. Together they raced to homeroom.

That afternoon, the first thing Corey noticed in Leila's extremely neat bedroom was an extremely messy stack of cardboard boxes marked Toxic by the door. The second thing was a photo she had propped up in her window. He kept his eyes on the photo intently, not wavering his gaze. This was mainly because Leila was busy clearing away all the underwear she had left on her bed. And those were the last things Corey wanted to see.

"Are you done yet?" he asked, trying to keep his face from turning red.

"Almost."

The photo was practically burning itself into his eyes now. It was sitting on Leila's old windowsill, which was chipped and cracked. Each of those cracks revealed several layers of paint. You could tell the age of the building with those layers, like rings of a tree. But the photo was frozen in time, black-and-white and maybe five inches by seven.

It was a New York City street scene. In the fore-ground was a dirt road with telegraph poles. To the far left, a small team of men was building a stone wall along that road. In the background, a hilly, treeless landscape stretched to the horizon. Here and there were signs of a construction project, like a team of horses pulling an enormous boulder on a flatbed cart. At the right was a wood-frame contraption about two stories tall, with a system of pulleys.

It was pretty blurry, but there was something both eerie and familiar about the image. He picked it up off the window to look closer. "Leila," he said, "what's this—?"

"Ta-da!" Leila's voice interrupted his question. "Which one should I wear?"

Corey turned around. Leila was holding up a Cat-woman and a Wonder Woman costume. "Whichever fits, I guess," he replied. "I like them both."

Leila sighed. "You are such a boy. Okay, get out of here while I change. And don't steal my auntie Flora's photo."

"I met her, right?" Corey asked. "She brought that weird musical instrument to your Christmas party—the dirigible?"

"Didgeridoo. Made from a bamboo pole. Yes. She finds stuff like that. She disappears for days or weeks at a time and never says where she's been. She also says she talks to dead people. Mostly you have to tune her out. Those boxes stacked by my door? Her stuff."

"And this photo?" Corey asked. "Is it—?"

"A view of Central Park? Yeah. Auntie Flora finds old photos that she feels some kind of weird mystical connection to. She thinks that one was probably taken in this exact room back in the 1860s, when they were constructing the park. That's why there are no trees. This apartment building was new then."

"Wow . . . ," Corey said. "She sounds awesome."

Leila shrugged. "Well, she left my uncle Lazslo months ago, no explanation. None of us knew where she went. When she finally wrote my uncle, she said she couldn't come back. 'Just know that I love you, I love you all,' she wrote. He's devastated and angry, and he wanted to toss all her junk. That's why he wrote Toxic on it. It's not really toxic. Anyway, my mom thinks they'll work it out. She claims Lazslo and Flora have a healthier relationship than she and Dad did. So she told my uncle not to throw it out. 'I know—let's store it in Leila's room!' she said. Imagine my surprise. Grrrrr. You want any of it?"

"Your aunt's old-lady stuff? I don't think so." Corey eyed the boxes, which were sealed except the top one. It had been opened roughly and the side was torn. An old framed photograph had fallen out, so Corey stooped to pick it up. As he tried to place it back in, he stopped.

The image was odd. At first glance it was just a group of about twelve people in stiff, old-fashioned clothing. Most of them were staring unsmilingly at the camera. But among them were a fluffy polar bear, a kangaroo, and a small triceratops. All looking very civilized.

Printed across the bottom of the photo was a title:

KNICKERBOCKERS
APRIL 1914

"I guess people had strange senses of humor back then," Corey said. "Those are really convincing costumes. What was her mystical connection to this photo?"

"What?" Leila said.

"You told me she had connections to all her photos."

"Oh." Leila peered at it briefly. "I think she collected this one because one of the old ladies in the picture looks like her."

"Maybe it is her." Corey shoved the framed photo back in the box.

"In 1914?"

Corey shrugged. "Maybe she left your uncle because she's dating a man her age—two hundred years old."

"Are you dissing my aunt, Corey Fletcher?" Leila snapped.

As Corey slipped out the door, giggling, he caught a Catwoman mask in the back of his head. "I'm having second thoughts about being your date tonight!" Leila shouted.

"It's not a date!" Corey shouted back.

Still holding on to the black-and-white photo, he ducked into the bathroom next to Leila's room. The window, which overlooked Central Park, was slightly open.

On the margin of the photo, someone had written the date OCT 1862. He stared at it. That date rang a bell for Corey, and it took a moment to figure out why.

He unbuckled his belt, the one Papou had left him. Checking the back of the buckle, he glanced at the stamped-in date: Oct 31, 1862.

The exact same vintage.

"Cool . . . ," he murmured.

He kneeled on the toilet for a better angle, shoved the window higher up, and stared at the view of the park across the street. It was so foggy, Corey could only see vague shapes. He could barely even make out the park's stone wall.

He loved when the fog got thick like this. You could imagine that you were in the wilderness. Or at least the country. Or the suburbs. To a New Yorker, the suburbs could be pretty exotic.

Corey balanced the photo on the windowsill. He looked from the photo to the scene across the street, and back again. In his mind, he tried to superimpose the photo image on the thick fog—the stonecutter kneeling by the half-built wall, the crane and the con-traption in the background.

Somebody flushed the toilet in the apartment above, and the lights flickered. Corey smiled. Old apartment buildings were so quirky. Across the street, the particles of fog seemed to swirl. They thickened and gathered on a howling wind. In the distance Corey heard thunder again. *There.* It wasn't fake after all. This time he was sure Leila could hear it, too. He watched the swirls of fog forming a shape, rising, squaring off. He saw a big derrick through the mist. That seemed a little weird. But not really. They were always renovating the playground.

Now a man emerged from the cloud, wearing a cap and baggy pants and smoking a cigarette. He sank to his knees, lifted a trowel from the sidewalk, and stuck it into a metal container. Corey blinked. *That* was something he hadn't seen. Had the container been there all along?

Now the guy was slathering mortar on a stone block. It was pretty strange. The dude really did look like the guy in the image.

Corey glanced down for the photo, to compare. It was no longer on the windowsill, so he looked toward the bathroom floor.

The breath caught in his throat. The floor was wooden and sagging in the middle. He could have sworn it had been tiled. The toilet had a tank overhead with a pull cord. He hadn't noticed that either.

"Leila . . . ?" he called out.

He heard voices out the window. Across the street, another man shuffled into view. His clothes were old and ragged, his beard long and gray. The man stopped to watch the stonemason for a moment, and then struck up a conversation.

Corey kneeled, sticking his head out a little further, trying to hear them. To his right, farther down Central Park West, came the distant clang of a bell. The two men laughed, and the older guy turned to go. As he waved good-bye, he looked over his shoulder. "Ta-ta!" he shouted. "Don't take any wooden nickels!"

Corey froze.

That phrase. He only knew one person who said it.

As the man turned again, Corey could see his face clearer. Through the soupy thickness of the fog he recognized the deep-set eyes. The long nose and cleft chin.

He shoved the window as high up as it would go.

"PAPOU!" he shouted at the top of his lungs. He expected his voice to be swallowed up in the city noise, but it echoed loud and clear across the empty street. "UP HERE!"

The old man looked startled. He glanced around, confused. Corey called again, waving his arms until finally the man looked up. His eyes met Corey's for a split second.

With a loud clang, a trolley rolled up Central Park West. It came to a noisy stop at the curb, directly in front of the man who looked like Papou.

Corey turned. From somewhere in the apartment a voice called out, but he didn't know or care who it was. He went to grab the doorknob, but there was none, just a black metal latch. Jamming it downward, he ran out of the bathroom.

He crashed straight into a short but stocky woman he'd never seen before, wearing an apron and clunky black shoes.

The woman let out a scream. Corey pivoted and ran for Leila's door. "Open up!" he shouted.

He pushed the door open. Inside, another strange woman, with a craggy face and silver hair, jumped out of a rocking chair and let out an even louder scream.

Corey turned, ran for the front door, and didn't look back.

5

The second thing Corey noticed, as he burst out of the building and onto Central Park West, was that the old man was gone.

The first thing was piles of horse manure on both sides of the road. He looked up and down the street, his chest heaving. Papou was nowhere in sight. The Walk sign was gone, too, as well as all streetlights and cars. The blacktop road was hard-packed gravel, and the silence was overwhelming.

He turned back to Leila's building. It was always the runt of the block, wedged between high-rises. Leila called it "the Little House" after her favorite picture book. Now it was the tallest building in sight. The great Central Park West towers were gone. All the way up into Harlem, and down to Columbus Circle, was a hodgepodge of low-rise brick buildings, shacks, and empty space.

"I need a shrink . . . ," Corey murmured. "I need a shrink. . . ."

There was a name for this condition, having delusions and believing them to be true. But he'd forgotten it. People like him ended up ranting in the streets to imaginary enemies. They sat muttering in the subways.

He never thought his senses could lie to him, but they could and they had. He smelled the manure that the horses had left in the street and the burning of wood in fireplaces. He saw sky in places he'd never seen it and heard the quiet of a city without machines. It all seemed so real.

Corey felt woozy. His stomach churned, like he'd been in the car too long. He staggered across the street. Behind him he heard the crack of a whip and a horse's whinny. "Get out of the way, ya drunken rascal!" a gravelly voice shouted.

He jumped onto the sidewalk, narrowly avoiding a horse-drawn coach.

"*You're not real!*" he shouted.

Tripping over the uneven pavement, Corey fell

against the park's stone wall. He glanced up as a windowed coach made of dark polished wood rolled by. A white-gloved hand pushed aside the window curtains, and a wrinkle-faced man in a top hat glowered at him.

"You're not real either," Corey muttered.

"Hmmf," the old man sniffed.

From Corey's left, a softer voice called out, "You okay, fella?"

Corey looked. A guy in a loose gray workman's uniform was on his knees, holding on to a stone with a gloved hand, about ten feet farther down the wall.

The stonemason.

"You—you were in the photo!" Corey blurted, hopping to his feet. "From the eighteen hundreds!"

With a snort, the guy turned around to another worker and made a circle sign with his index finger on the side of his head. *Cuckoo.*

Corey slumped on a park bench. It hadn't yet been bolted to the sidewalk, so he and the bench teetered backward. Out of the corner of his eye, he noticed a white envelope slipping off the seat and falling to the ground.

He lifted it and looked at the writing:

For Buster Squires

His hand began to shiver. Then his whole body. It was Papou's nickname for him.

Steady, Corey, he thought. *Go with it. It will all fade away and you'll snap out of this.*

Whatever this is.

"Son? You lost or something?"

Corey barely registered the stonemason's voice. He ripped the top off the envelope and pulled out a message.

```
D U M B W A I T E R
D E L I V E R S
1 T 0 2 6

I N A P
O R T H E
N I N T H
W O R D Y
F O O D S
C A S E M E
```

Graph paper. Just like Papou used all the time. Their house was full of graph paper. All his life Papou had been an engineer. He'd buy pads and pads of it.

"I'm not seeing this . . . ," Corey said.

The stonemason was standing next to him now, looking warily over his shoulder. "Looks important.

You got a marriage proposal in the mail?"

"My grandfather," Corey replied.

"A marriage proposal from your *grandfather?*"

"No!"

Don't talk, Corey said to himself. *He is not real. This is your imagination.*

Corey envisioned himself as the real world must be seeing him—sitting on a park bench, talking to no one. He watched suspiciously as the man leaned to look at the note. "You are a delusion," Corey said. "A figment."

"Nope, an Italian. Lorenzo Scotto." He stuck out his hand and Corey shook it. It felt real, all right. Like a slab of granite. "Looks like you got some kind of riddle there, kid. Your grandpa likes riddles?"

Corey closed his eyes for a few seconds, thinking this all might disappear. No such luck. Lorenzo stayed put.

"He likes codes," Corey murmured. "Puzzles. He taught me to do the *New York Times* Sunday crossword puzzle."

"I don't read the *Times*. Maybe I should. I'm a *Frank Leslie* kind of guy." Lorenzo reached into his back pocket and pulled out a tabloid newspaper, slapping it down on the bench next to the discarded envelope. "Good to meet you . . . Buster."

The masthead of Lorenzo's newspaper said *Frank*

Leslie's Illustrated Newspaper. The front page was full of garish hand-drawn scenes—stabbings, fat men in top hats, monster-like people attacking helpless rich folk.

But Corey barely noticed those.

He stared at the date on the top of the front page: October 31, 1862

A breeze wafted by his face, carrying scents of dirt, manure, rotting leaves—and newspaper print. Corey felt numb. "Tell me this isn't real."

Lorenzo laughed. "Well, you know *Frank's*, they can flower up a story."

"No, I mean all of it. I mean the date," Corey said. "Is it really October thirty-first, 1862?"

"That's what I say, too. Hoo-eee, October already! Seems like it was summer just yesterday!"

"That's not what I meant." Corey sank back into the bench again. He looked Lorenzo straight in the eye. "It is 1862. It really is. I'm not crazy. There are no cars, right? Or telephones. There's a war down South. *And my grandfather is here all alone, trying to tell me something!* Is this all true?"

Lorenzo shrugged. "Well, you're making sense to me. Can I ask you a question? I know times is tough. Your grandpa, ain't he got a place to live?"

"Well . . . I don't know. He left home and never contacted anyone. So maybe yes. Maybe no."

"That's why he's using code, then. Doesn't want nobody to find him but you. Prob'ly got his reasons. Nowadays you never know why people do the things they do. Anyway, them constables, they're liable to throw him in jail for vagrancy." The man smiled. "Hey, I'll help you if you want. I may be Italian, but I'm good at puzzles."

Corey cocked his head curiously. "What does being Italian have to do with that?"

Lorenzo shrugged. "Ahh, you know, the hoity-toity, they all think we're a bunch of monkeys with no brains. They want to build a park on this land, right? Bang, they kick us out of our houses—us, the Poles, the Africans, the Irish. Businesses, churches, gone. Now all the swells can have a place to show off their carriages. And whaddaya know, all the land around the park gets expensive, too! Right where they're buying up land. What a surprise!"

"It will get worse," Corey murmured. "Apartments for a hundred million dollars."

"Lucky us, we get to build this stone wall around the park," Lorenzo barreled on. "And then we go home to little shacks where they can't see us. Someday this will change. Now show me that puzzle before I get too angry to think."

Corey held out the sheet to the man.

"'Dumbwaiter delivers one to twenty-six,'" Lorenzo read aloud. "Okay, I'm going to put some spaces in the next words, or it don't make no sense. 'I nap, or the ninth wordy foods case me.' See, I read pretty good!"

"But that doesn't make sense," Corey pointed out.

"Yeah, good pernt," Lorenzo agreed.

"Pernt?" Corey said. "You mean *point*?"

"'Swhat I said. Pernt. Okay, let's start with the dumbwaiter and work our way down." Lorenzo widened his eyes like a bad standup comic holding for a laugh. "Ha! See what I did there?"

"Right . . . dumbwaiter . . . work our way down . . ." Corey forced himself to concentrate. "But doesn't a dumbwaiter carry things up *and* down—like an elevator?"

"An ele-*what*?" Lorenzo asked.

"Right, maybe they haven't been invented yet," Corey said. "So, yeah. Dumbwaiter. And the one to twenty-six, that could be floors of a building."

Lorenzo laughed. "That'd be some building! The walls would have to be a mile thick to hold the weight.

You know what I think? We gotta look at the top part of this code first. It's some kind of way to understand the bottom. A kind of . . . whaddaya call it—?"

"Key!" Corey replied.

"Key."

"Uh-huh," Corey said. "So the top part of the message is telling us to decode the bottom by carrying something up and down. . . ."

"Like a dumbwaiter . . . ," Lorenzo murmured. "But why 'one to twenty-six'?"

Corey thought a moment. "It's twice thirteen. Twice the bad luck."

"There's also twenty-six letters in the alphabet." Lorenzo pointed to his head. "I remember that from school."

"Yes! What if 'one to twenty-six' is a way of saying the letters go up and down?" With Lorenzo looking over his shoulder, Corey focused on the bottom part of the message. "So if we read these letters vertically in each column . . ."

He silently read the columns of letters, top to bottom: NWFC IOIOOA NRNROS ATTDDE PHHYSM E E.

"I don't think so," Lorenzo said. "Unless that's Greek or something."

Bottom-to-top was nonsense, too.

"Okay, okay, we can get this . . . ," Corey said. "Could be it's not about reading up and down. A dumb-waiter . . . moves stuff."

"We knew that."

"From floor to floor."

"We knew that, too."

"Maybe that's what we're supposed to do, Lorenzo—move the letters. Like a word scramble, but vertical instead of horizontal."

Lorenzo scratched his head. "That first column is N, W, F, C. No matter how you scramble that, it ain't nothing. No vowels."

"Yeah, but what about rearranging vertically, and then reading what you get horizontally?" Corey said.

"This is getting complicated," Lorenzo said.

"Papou always told me, when you think it's impossible, 'Look for something you recognize.' . . ."

Lorenzo scratched his chin. "Well, this is a note to you, right? Maybe your name is in it. Like, hidden."

Corey stared at the graph paper. C in Column 1, O in Column 2, R in Column 3 . . . "I think I see it."

Lorenzo pulled a pencil from behind his ear. "Need this?"

The pencil was greasy and chewed up, but Corey

didn't care. Taking it from Lorenzo, he began re-arranging:

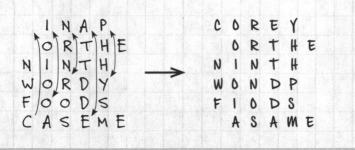

"I thought your name was Buster," Lorenzo said.

"It's a nickname. Corey's my real name."

"Well, razzamatazza! Hey, now I'm seeing another word—*woods!*"

Corey saw it, too:

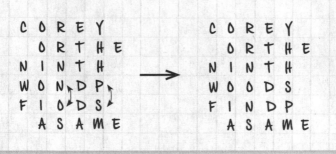

Corey's eyes widened as he stared at the bottom two lines.

"I see find," he said. "And I see me. 'Find me'!"

"Like I said, the guy is scared," Lorenzo whispered. "He don't want no one to see you meeting him in public."

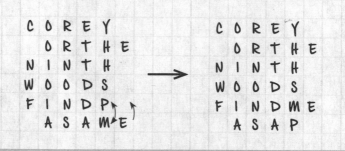

FIND ME ASAP.

That did not sound good. Sweat gathered on Corey's scalp as he began fixing the rest of it.

Finally he made one small rearrangement to get the message.

```
C O R E Y              C O R E Y
  I N T H E            F I N D M E
N O R T H                I N T H E
W O O D S              N O R T H
F I N D M E            W O O D S
  A S A P                A S A P
```

"He needs me!" Corey blurted out, his chest thumping.

"Smart guy," Lorenzo said. "If somebody besides you picked this up, they wouldn't know where he was. I'm reading it, and I don't know. Where's the North Woods?"

"Nowhere now. It's where it will be," Corey said. "The top of the park—like, a hundredth to a hundredth and tenth streets. They left it—I mean, the park designers are planning to leave it like a forest."

He bolted up from the bench and stuffed the note in his pocket, quickly shaking Lorenzo's hand. "Thanks for your help."

Lorenzo smiled but didn't let go. "Wait. Maybe you can help me now. Just one question. Who the heck are you, and how do you know so much about things that haven't been invented and what's going to happen with the park? I may not be too smart, but I want the truth. And don't worry. I keep secrets."

Corey locked eyes with the man. He believed that Lorenzo kept secrets. He also believed the man was very smart. And Lorenzo deserved the truth, as crazy as it should sound.

"I—I'm from the future," he said. "I traveled in time."

Lorenzo's bushy eyebrows collided at the top of his nose. "Yeah? How?"

"I'm not sure. It has something to do with a locket and a belt buckle, I think." Corey took a deep breath. "You think I'm nuts, right?"

Lorenzo shook his head. "I read *Frank Leslie* every week. There's all kind of weird stuff goes on in this world."

"So you actually believe me?" Corey asked.

Behind Lorenzo, another workman was clearing his throat. "Hey, hate to break up the party, your highness, but there's woik to do," he grumbled.

"Shut yer trap, be right there," Lorenzo replied.

He gave Corey a long, hard look. "I don't know if I believe you. You're dressed like nobody I ever seen, you use woids I never hoid of before, so I don't know what to make of you. But I told you I kept secrets, and I'm a man of my woid."

Corey edged backward. "Well, I appreciate it. So—"

"Just a sec." Lorenzo stepped up close to Corey. "What if you are telling the truth? Just for grins, can I ask you another question? Just between you and me?"

"Sure," Corey said. "Whatever."

"I don't believe I'm asking this." Lorenzo took a deep breath. He shook his head and muttered something in Italian that sounded like a prayer. "Tell me, Future Boy, does the country survive the War Between the States?"

"It will be called the Civil War," Corey replied. "And, yes."

"No joke?" Lorenzo's left eyebrow arched skeptically.

"Abraham Lincoln signs an emancipation proclamation, the slaves are freed, and the South joins the North as one country. It gets really complicated after that, but . . . yeah."

The man's eyes grew moist. "Bless you, big guy," he said. "Your grandfather is a lucky man."

6

Leila caught a strange burning smell from the bathroom's closed door. "Corey, what are you smoking
in there?"

She knocked politely, then harder. Corey was not
responding.

She'd begun to sweat the moment she put on
her Catwoman costume, and this was making things
worse. She gripped the doorknob and shook it. "Ready
or not, here I come."

Slowly she opened the door. The light was still on,
but Corey was nowhere to be seen. Leila's eyes focused
on the window, which was wide open.

She raced to the window in a panic. He'd been

nervous, afraid he was losing his mind. Had he . . . ?

They were only on the second floor. If he had done something awful, he might still be lucky—a broken leg, maybe. Kneeling on the toilet, she stuck her head out the window and looked down. "*Corey!*" she screamed.

She looked up and down Central Park West, but there was no sign of him.

"Mo-o-o-om, have you seen Corey?" she shouted, running out of the room.

She could hear her mother's desk chair rolling back on the wood floor of her home office just behind the kitchen. The Sharps' apartment was long and narrow, with all rooms opening into one long hallway. So it took about two seconds for Jessie Sharp to come padding out of the little room by the kitchen and into the hallway. Leila could tell she'd been up most of the night writing. In her photo for her syndicated newspaper column, Sharp Eyes on Washington, Mom looked like Natalie Portman, all elegant and glamorous and put together. Schlepping out of the office in her purple sweats after a long day, she looked like an extra on *The Walking Dead*. "Heyyy, the costume looks great, sweetie—"

"Mom, Corey was in the bathroom and now I can't

find him," Leila said. "Did you see him leave?"

Leila's mom shook her head. "Nope. I mean, I guess I should have seen him if he did. My office door was open. But maybe not. I'm a little distracted with dead-lines. Keep looking, Leila. He might have snuck out to put on his costume. Or he's hiding, pranking you. You know Corey."

Leila raced back down the hallway. She opened the small linen closet in the wall next to the bathroom. She pulled back the shower curtain and checked in the cab-inet under the sink. Sitting at the edge of the bathtub, Leila looked at her phone, but there were no new texts from him.

That was when she saw the upside-down photo on the bathroom floor. She stooped to pick it up, and she turned it over. It was the black-and-white image she'd had on her windowsill, from Auntie Flora's collection. She'd seen it a hundred times—the half-finished stone wall, the barren road under construction, the vast and featureless park, the crane.

But something was off.

The construction worker—the guy building the wall—wasn't in the place she remembered him. In the photo, he'd been kneeling near the center, putting mortar on a block of stone.

Leila's jaw dropped open. Now, in the photo, the block was resting on the ground. That same worker was sitting on a park bench, talking to a kid.

And the kid looked exactly like Corey Fletcher.

7

On an ordinary day, Corey could run the paths of Central Park with his eyes closed. But not on an ordinary day in 1862. And not without the paths.

He was used to maple trees and squirrels and pigeons. Joggers and bikers and skaters. Old people with walkers, toddlers in strollers. But Central Park in 1862 had none of these. The big reservoir was a dusty field. Everything else was a mix of scraggly bushes, giant rocks, and tree stumps. On the Ninety-Seventh Street transverse road, which cut through the park, horse-pulled carts groaned with the weight of fruits and vegetables. The road was sunken into a wide trench, but on the overpass Corey could look down and see horseback riders weaving in and out like motorbikers. Children ran ahead of their mothers and fathers, laughing, sneaking an apple or two from the carts while their parents weren't looking. Cart horses bucked, their drivers shaking fists and shouting insults at each other. Corey had to hold his nose against the stink of manure, rotting food, and body odor.

On the other side of the overpass, he ran over hills of chapped soil and scrubby grass. The park was unrecognizable. His favorite willow-shaded lake on the left, close to Central Park West and One Hundredth Street, was a marshy swamp. The baseball fields to his right were a barren plain. But Corey's eyes were drawn to the dense forest beyond the plain, where trees rose to the sky above a shadowy valley. There, north of One Hundredth Street, the park construction hadn't yet begun. Soon the landscapers would move in, dynamiting rocks, creating paths, redirecting streams, to make the North Woods.

Now it was just . . . woods. Real woods, not replanted and reshaped by humans.

FIND ME IN THE NORTH WOODS ASAP.

This had to be the place.

Corey followed the streambed into the forest and

ran down a slope toward a waterfall. The fog swirled in and out of the pines, and shadows moved among the bushes.

"Papou!" he cried out.

His voice fell flat in the thick fog. At the top of a waterfall, he stopped and looked over the ravine below.

On the left bank, a dark, hooded figure emerged from behind a tree. The person was crouched low to the ground, holding a branch that tapered to a sharp point like a spear.

It could have been Papou, but the face was hidden within the hood's shadow. Corey stepped off the bridge and onto the sloping bank. As he climbed down toward the stream, the cracking of branches underfoot made the figure look up.

There was no mistaking his grandfather's eyes. The old man smiled briefly, then held up an index finger to his mouth in a shushing gesture. He pointed toward the bottom of the waterfall. Corey slowed, trying to keep his footfalls silent.

The falls cascaded over a pile of granite boulders to land in a churning pool. The water was rougher than it was in the present, the stream wider. At the base of the waterfall, something moved between the boulders. Something large. With gray, coarse fur.

Corey slowed down. To his right, Papou was edging closer. "*Proseche*," he whispered.

Corey's breath caught in his throat. That was Greek for "be careful"—something Papou said a million times to him when he was a kid. The old man planted his feet and let loose with the stick spear. It hurtled through the air and landed in the stream, inches from its target. Hearing the splash, the creature flinched in its crevice. Branches hid its face from Corey's sight, but its haunches were wiggling, its legs digging into the muck. Its body was longer than a rat's, thicker than a beaver's.

Slowly it moved into sight, its eyes beady and rimmed with red. Its mouth seemed to be drawn into a smile along either side of a long snout. At the base of the snout, two white tusks curved upward like some kind of giant warthog's.

Its eyes moved from Papou to Corey and back again. "Well, well," it said. "There are two of you."

Corey shrieked. He jumped back, tripping over a tangle of branches. His grandfather charged past him, his fist closed around a large, sharp rock. "Run, Corey!" he bellowed.

"It—it . . . ," Corey stammered.

"Do as I say, *paithaki mou!*" the old man said. "Turn

around and run—now! I will join you!"

Corey sprang to his feet and scrambled up the slope. He ran as fast as he could, pushing aside branches, looking for a path. Further upstream, he spotted a dark figure in the woods. "Hey!" he cried out! *"Help!"*

He was answered by a gunshot.

Corey leaped back, tumbling down the hill. He managed to stop himself before reaching the water and held himself low to the ground. Had that person just shot at *him?* What on earth was going on here?

Crawling behind thick bushes, Corey held still. He couldn't go back and he didn't want to go forward. He glanced over his shoulder for Papou, but that part of the woods was swallowed in fog. Ahead, the sharp smell of burned gunpowder wafted toward him. A thin blackish plume of smoke rose through the fog into the tree canopies, but the dark figure was on the ground, moaning.

Quietly Corey crept uphill to another set of bushes, then ran behind a thick oak tree. From his vantage point now, he could see a revolver lying on the forest floor. The man's chest was moving. He was still alive. Instinctively Corey reached into his pocket for his phone, but that wasn't going to do him much good here.

"Hey!" Corey called out. "Are—are you okay?"

As the body twitched, Corey pocketed his phone and backed away slowly. He could see the face now, a white guy with soot-stained cheeks and bloodshot, steely blue eyes. "You . . . fool," he murmured. "Why did you do that?"

"Do what?" Corey asked.

"Shout like that." The guy was standing now. Patches of unmatched material held his clothes together, and the outfit looked like it hadn't seen a washing machine in years. "Why did you stop me from what I intended to do?"

"From k-k-killing yourself?" Corey asked.

The young man scooped the gun off the ground. His eyes were wild as he ran forward. Corey backed away but the guy was fast.

"You do it," he said, shoving the revolver toward him.

"Do what?" Corey asked.

The man forced the gun into Corey's hand. It was an old-fashioned revolver and felt like it weighed a hundred pounds. "Shoot me!"

"What? No! No!"

The man stepped back, his hands stretched outward. "Do it. From the looks of you, you may be in my place soon."

"Look, I don't know what you're talking about," Corey said. "I—I don't live here. Well, I *do*, technically, but—"

"Are you a rich man's son?"

"No!"

The guy let out a crazed, wild-eyed laugh. "I didn't think so. The government paid my parents three hundred and fifty dollars so I could go to war—in the place of some banker's son. This is how it works, lad. The wealthy buy their way out. Me, I'd rather die here near Montanye's Rivulet than on a field by a rebel's musket for another man's convenience. And that makes me a deserter, boy. Which means it is your duty to shoot me!"

"*Papou!*" Corey shouted down into the fog.

Behind him, at the top of the slope, came the sound of clopping hooves. The bearded guy trained his eyes upward. Perched on horses, a pair of scowling men with handlebar mustaches came into view along the road above. They wore strapped helmets and tight woolen uniforms with clubs tucked into their belts.

"Excuse me, chaps," one of them called down, "are you thinking this is perhaps the Oregon Trail? Some grassy plain where buffalo roam and wild gunfire is the order of the day?"

"No, sir," Corey grumbled.

"Constable Bromley to you, lad," the man said, "and this is my jolly partner, Constable Moosup."

Moosup's face, a shade of orange to begin with, was growing red. His eyes looked ready to spring out of his head. "*NAMES!*" he demanded.

"Frederick Ruggles," muttered the young bearded guy.

"Corey Fletcher," Corey piped up.

"Well then, now that we are acquainted, kindly put that revolver away, Fletcher, and don't let us hear another shot!" Bromley replied. "Because unless we have frightfully lost our way, this is most certainly New York City. Where hunting is strictly forbidden."

"*NOW!*" Moosup bellowed.

Awkwardly Corey shoved the revolver into his pocket. It was a miracle his pants didn't fall to his ankles. It was even more of a miracle he didn't shoot his own leg off. "Done," he said.

Bromley was eyeing Corey intently. "Now then, gentlemen, perhaps you may help us. We are on the way to investigate an incident on the Eighth Avenue, not far from here. Seems a young man, by unlawful entry, compromised the honor and privacy of a young lady in her apartment dwelling. Emerged from the toilet, to be exact. This upsets me very much, but Constable Moosup even more so, as he is . . . erm, familiar with said young lady."

Moosup growled.

"Don't know what you're talking about," Frederick grumbled.

Bromley pulled out a small pocket notebook from his jacket and read from it. "Tall, very thin, perhaps fifteen years of age—"

"Thirteen," Corey said.

"Oh?" Bromley said.

Moosup's eyes bore down on Corey like smoldering flames.

"I mean, I'm thirteen!" Corey blurted. "So I couldn't be the same person who was hiding in the bathroom!"

"You craven little . . ." Moosup hopped off his horse. He looked about seven feet tall. As he stomped down the slope toward Corey, he reached for a wooden club attached to his belt.

Frederick Ruggles moved in front of Corey, blocking his path. "Now see here, Constable Moose Cup!"

As the big man roared, raising the club high over his head, Corey reached into his pocket and pulled out the revolver. He hadn't the slightest idea how to hold it, let alone use it. But he gripped it tight with both hands and pointed it at the charging constable. *"Leave him alone!"*

Constable Bromley gasped. Moosup stood frozen with the club aloft.

"That," Frederick Ruggles said, looking at Corey with astonishment, "may not have been your wisest choice."

Corey gulped. He felt a pinpoint of heat in the center of his chest. But Moosup was looking at something over Corey's shoulder.

A sharp crackling of branches came from behind him. *Papou.* Corey turned, taking his eye from the two constables. In that moment Moosup lunged for him. As Corey tried to pull the revolver away, he felt the weight of the giant man knock him to the ground. With the dexterity of someone smaller and lighter, Moosup snatched away the gun.

Corey rolled and then sprang to his feet, hands in the air. The revolver firmly gripped in both hands, Moosup pointed its barrel at Corey's forehead. "Yer friend was correct," he said. "Now do as I say or I'll . . ."

But his voice trailed off, as his eyes focused on something over Corey's shoulder.

"Drop that," snapped a deep, booming voice. It was close behind Corey, and it didn't sound like Papou.

Corey turned. As a shadow grew in the fog's whiteness, he stiffened.

"Sweet mother of Goshen . . . ," Moosup whispered.

Corey had seen the creature before, but as it crawled out of the whiteness Corey's hair stood on end. The thing was shaped like a warthog but its face was lower to the ground, its legs bent to the sides. Its tusks glistened in the moisture, and drool dripped from either side of its barrel-like snout. It crawled forward steadily, eyes fixed on Moosup, its breath chuffing like a train.

Frederick Ruggles turned and ran up the slope, screaming. Both horses bucked and whinnied. Constable Bromley held tight to his, but Moosup's went galloping away. "*Moosup, run!*" Bromley cried out.

Moosup dropped the revolver and backed away. With a roar, the creature leaped. The constable sprang into the air and ran up toward Bromley, who was leaning from the saddle, his hand outstretched.

Bromley's horse was having none of it and dashed away at a full gallop. Roaring in fear, Moosup sprinted along behind it, down the hill toward One Hundredth Street.

As the creature thundered past Corey, he turned back toward the creek. At the bottom of the slope, Papou emerged from the fog, hurrying toward him.

"You did it!" he said, wrapping him in a tight hug.

"Did what?" Corey said. "It was that—that thing. It chased them away."

"I meant, you wore the belt buckle. I knew you'd find it."

"Belt? My *belt*? I wear it all the time, Papou, but what does that have to do with—?"

"Sshhh." Papou was looking up the hill. Corey could hear the beast snuffling, but it was invisible in the fog.

The two ran back down the hill and along the stream bank, scrabbling over rock outcroppings. They leaped across a narrow part of the stream and up the other bank. "Do you have money?" Papou shouted.

"Money?"

"Coins, *paithaki*! Something metal from the present time."

The old man stopped running and turned. Corey reached into his pocket, pulling out fifty-seven cents. "Spare change, yeah, but—"

"Hold tight to it, Corey," Papou said. "You need that to get back. And you need to go now."

"Coins . . . the locket . . . the belt buckle . . ." Corey shook his head in wonder and confusion. "Okay. Okay. So *that's* the secret to time travel, Papou? *Metal?*"

"We will talk another time," Papou said.

"No, we have to talk now! There's so much I don't understand. I thought you went to Canada—"

"Corey, you're in danger. You must go back now."

"How does it work?" Corey demanded. "Like, hold some metal and, zoom, you're gone? Or do you have to do something, like click your heels three times and say 'There's no place like home'? You have to tell me, Papou. I'm scared!"

A muffled roar sounded from the ravine. A sloppy splash. Two red eyes pierced the gloom like lanterns.

Papou took Corey's left hand. With his right, Corey grabbed tight to the coins. They burned to the touch, and the sky opened into a burst of harsh white light.

8

Leila's mom swallowed a mouthful of sausage and pepperoni pizza before commenting on Leila's photo. "Yes, it does look a lot like Corey. But Corey's got that kind of face."

Leila looked up from the photo, which she had placed on the kitchen table. "What does that mean? *What* kind of face?"

"He has an old-fashioned look," her mom replied. "A lot of kids in these vintage photos have a Corey-like look. Also the way he talks, kind of formal and old-school. He's like a throwback to another time."

"That's not the point, Mom," Leila insisted. "There *was* no kid in this photo before. Then Corey took it from me, went into the bathroom, disappeared, and the next thing I know, I find this!"

Her mom laughed. "So my logical daughter is thinking he disappeared and—poof!—transported himself magically into the photo?"

"Well, what do you think?"

"Leila, you know I've run into a lot of professional pranksters in my journalistic career. I'm thinking there's probably a series of photos like this in Auntie Flora's collection, all taken from the same spot. Nineteenth-century photography involved complicated cameras on tripods. Lots of effort involved. So maybe, if you're a photographer, you don't just take one photo, but a bunch over time. Knowing Corey, he saw the photo on your window and then he saw this one in the box. It's pretty much identical, but obviously taken a few minutes *after* the window photo. He probably thought it was pretty funny to see this kid who looked like him. So he pocketed the window photo, then snuck this one into the bathroom and left it for you to find. He figured he'd freak you out."

"That's pretty elaborate," Leila remarked.

Her mom laughed. "You don't think Corey Fletcher is capable of elaborate pranks?"

"Good point," Leila said, ripping off a slice of pizza.

"Well, it worked. And when I see him at the party, he is toast."

"Go for it, Catwoman," Mom said. "Meow, hiss."

Leila wolfed down a slice, swigged some seltzer, and ran back to her room. Placing her Catwoman mask over her face, she looked in the mirror. Perfect, except for the stringy hair, which looked more like it belonged to Catfish-woman.

That wouldn't be too hard to fix.

One of Auntie Flora's cartons was full of weird barrettes and costume jewelry. Quickly Leila rooted around to find something appropriate. At the bottom of the carton was an old-fashioned Russian lacquer box, which she hadn't seen before. She lifted it out to set aside, but it was oddly warm to the touch. And exquisitely beautiful.

She held it to the light. On the lid was a bright-colored painting of a skating scene in a park. In the center was a luminous young skater with flaming red hair in midleap. She was surrounded by adoring men and looked a lot like Auntie Flora herself—which were probably the two reasons her aunt had bought the box. Auntie Flora loved collecting things where she could see "herself." Leila's shrink would call that narcissism.

The box was locked tight. It would have to wait for later. Leila set it back down, then grabbed from the carton an angular black barrette that looked vaguely catlike. Quickly she gathered her hair, clipped it back, and gave one last appraising glance.

It would do.

Racing out of the house, she took the stairs two at a time to the first floor. Waiting there were her two best friends, Rachel Eisen and Claudia Ramos. Rachel was dressed as Wonder Woman and Claudia wore a bulky costume with enormous black wings.

"Whoa . . . awesome outfit," Leila said. "Who are you?"

"Claudia," Claudia said.

"That's not funny," Rachel replied.

"The Angel of Death is not known for her sense of humor," Claudia said.

Leila pushed open the front door. Just outside the building, an enormous white-haired lump raised up onto four legs. It was definitely a cat of some kind, but it looked like one of its ancestors had mated with a terribly ugly badger. It stared at Leila and let out a low, rumbly noise halfway between a meow and a purr.

"Hey, Catsquatch is here!" Rachel cried out.

"Jabba the Cat!" Claudia added.

Everyone in the neighborhood had a name for this lurking creature. Its eyes were bugged out, its snout rough and protruding, almost like a dog's. No one seemed to know who it belonged to. It never really bothered anyone, but it gave Leila the creeps.

"Just my luck, I think it likes my costume," Leila said, shooing the cat away. "Let's go."

"Aren't you going to wait for your boyfriend?" Rachel asked.

"Corey, Corey, tell me a story," Claudia chimed.

"He's not my boyfriend," Leila said. "And I don't know where he is."

"I do," Claudia volunteered. "I just saw him, on my way here. When I was walking through the park? He was sitting on a bench near the willow pond. With somebody dressed as a homeless guy."

Leila turned in the doorway. "*What?* He said he was going with me—*us.*"

Claudia shrugged. "He didn't have his costume on yet."

Leila took a deep breath. Pranking her was bad enough. But pranking to avoid going to the party with her? That was really, really lame.

"You could go with Catsquatch," Rachel said.

"Hrrrrr . . ." Catsquatch growled.

"I'll meet you guys there," Leila said, barging through the front door. "I need to settle some business first."

Leaving Rachel and Claudia agape, she ran outside and headed for the park.

The blaring of taxi horns was like music to Corey.

He sat on a park bench, staring at the small commemorative steel plaque on the green wooden slat behind him: "Uncle Melvin's Special Central Park Spot. RIP 1934–2018." He didn't know who Uncle Melvin was but was grateful for his life. Because those dates meant Corey was now back to sometime after 2018.

Papou was explaining time travel. He must have been pretty good at it, because he'd followed Corey into the present. He was also talking a mile a minute, and Corey wasn't understanding a word.

After what had just happened, Corey's brain was mush. He felt like he'd just taken an overnight flight to New York from Mongolia. Or maybe from Neptune. "Can you start again," Corey said, "but slowly, like I'm a toddler? Whose first language is Swedish?"

The old man put his arm around Corey and sat back. Pointing to the sky, he said, "In a few hours, what will we see up there, *palikari mou*?"

The mist was beginning to lift. The sun had nearly set, giving the sky a muddy orange-gray hue. "Nothing."

"Nothing?"

"Well, it's foggy and it's New York City."

"Ah. But if we were in, say, the country?"

"Stars and planets."

Papou nodded. "Yes. Now, what if we were staring at a star, and at that moment a giant intergalactic force decided to blow it up. Then what would we see?"

"A big mess."

Papou shook his head. "We'd see nothing different. Because the light from that star takes a few thousand years to get here. What we're seeing now—that's the star as it *used* to be. We're looking directly into the past, Corey."

"That's a little mind-blowing." Corey squinted into the sky, even though there was nothing to see. "Okay, wait. So that star we're pretending to see—let's say it has a solar system, and that solar system has a planet like Earth. And I use this awesome super telescope to look at that planet. And I see this kid. He's got a telescope, too, and he's looking back. I wave. Does he wave back?"

"No," Papou said. "Because through *his* telescope, he's not seeing you. He's seeing what was here thousands of years ago. A forest with deer and bears. Maybe a native Lenni-Lenape family going to sleep. So there's the paradox. The moment we see him, he's actually long gone into dust, dead. At the same moment, from his perspective, none of us has been born yet! Einstein spent his life trying to figure this stuff out. He showed that time and space were elastic—that they could bend and fold in on themselves."

"I think I get that," Corey said. "Unless I think too hard. Then my head falls off."

"What we call the present is not just one moment," Papou went on. "It contains all the moments that came before. So it stands to reason we should be able to access some of them."

"And that's what we just did?" Corey murmured. "Down by the ravine?"

"Exactly," Papou said. "And we're not the only ones. Many other people do it, too. Some of them realize it, some don't. They assume they're dreaming, or they give it a convenient name. You know the phrase déjà vu?"

"Uh, duh, yeah," Corey replied. "As in, 'How weird is this, I feel like I've been here before'? That déjà vu? So, people who have that are time travelers?"

"Not all, but some," Papou said. "The whole thing

confused me at first. I tried to convince people I was having these . . . experiences. People said I had a crazy imagination. Ha. Sound familiar? Anyway, I didn't realize I could actually do it—really, really travel in time—until late in life, ten years ago. Now I'm pretty good at it. I've also had some support." Papou reached into his pocket and pulled out a card:

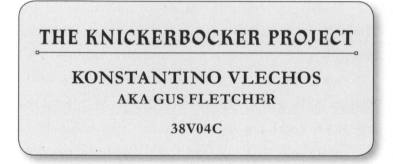

THE KNICKERBOCKER PROJECT

KONSTANTINO VLECHOS
AKA GUS FLETCHER

38V04C

"Knickerbocker . . . ," Corey said. "Wait. That was also the name of your book club, right?"

Papou took a deep breath, his lips tightening. "We *said* we were a book club, *paithaki*. We met every month. I was lucky to live in New York, where the group was based. Other members came from all over the world. They lied to their families about why they moved here. We didn't talk about books, Corey. We talked about our time hops, and we recorded notes in a log."

"Hops? Wait . . ." Corey pressed the tips of his fingers to each side of his head, as if to keep everything from blowing outward. "How does it happen? When I . . . hopped, and I saw you out Leila's bathroom window—how did you know I'd be there?"

"I left you the Civil War belt buckle for a reason," Papou replied. "Time-hopping can be unpredictable and random—equal parts genetics, art, and science."

"*Genetics?*" Corey said. "So . . . some people inherit diabetes, some inherit curly hair, and I inherited *time travel?*"

Papou laughed. "That is an incredibly simplified way of looking at it, but more or less . . . yes. But there are other necessary ingredients for it to occur. Most important is skin contact with a metal from the time period. Believe it or not, often a photograph alone will do, because of the silver content. The atomic structure of metals is different from other elements—rigid, solid, matrix-like. This is why they conduct electricity, and perhaps we will see someday how they help conduct time. You know I have another identical buckle. I was lucky to find a pair. The buckles' stamps reveal that they were was forged on October thirty-first, 1862. All I needed was one time hop to that date. And I waited."

Corey laughed with disbelief. "Wait, that's it? To

travel in time you just squeeze metal?"

"Well, no. When you travel by bicycle, you don't just sit on it and expect it to go where you need it to. There are other elements—awareness of your goal, desire to reach it."

"You have to want it."

"Exactly. There are triggers that can accelerate the action—physical or psychological danger, a strong dream or daydream. Adrenaline is a help. Time travel is as much physical as metaphysical."

"This is so incredible, Papou." Corey began pacing back and forth. "The possibilities are awesome. You could change so many things . . . like, go back and stop wars from happening. You could bomb Hitler, prevent assassinations—"

"No, no, not so fast." Papou smiled sadly. "Physical laws apply. Time is linear—meaning in a line. What happens happens. You can't change what occurred in the past, no matter what. Sure, there are alternate theories. Some believe multiple timelines exist, with differing events. Some think there have been very special humans capable of going from one to the other, allowing the timelines to leak. In effect, this would allow the events of one timeline to wipe out another. All very blah blah blah and hocus-pocus, if you ask me."

"How do you know?" Corey insisted.

"We certainly have tested it! Assassination, you say? I went to Ford's Theatre to save Abraham Lincoln. I knew what the assassin looked like, I had the date and time, but they threw me out because I didn't have a ticket. One thing about history—it *happened*. So whatever you try, you're destined to fail. Still, you always think you'll be the one. You think 'maybe next time.' So you go back. It can be addictive. I—I went many times to 2001 . . . to the day we lost your *yiayia*. . . ."

His voice drifted off.

The death of Corey's grandmother on 9/11 was something the family never really talked about. Corey slid closer to his grandfather and put an arm around his shoulder. "You tried to save her, Papou?" he said.

"I don't like to think about it," the old man said, turning away.

"You did, didn't you?"

The old man was motionless for a good minute, then nodded. "I failed again and again. I went to September eleventh. I also went to September eighth and September tenth. Every time, something different went wrong. On one of my time hops, I saw her in the crowd heading to work in the tower." Papou took a deep, sad breath. "One time I waited in the building. I pleaded with her, but I got too frantic. She misunderstood me. We'd been arguing that morning, and she blew past me. I was trying so hard, I just spooked her, I think. It took a long time for me to accept the truth—that I was helpless. It was as if she died four times. . . ."

"I don't blame you for trying," Corey said softly. "You had to. Maybe you should try again. I can come with you! It would be so cool to meet her. To *save* her!"

Papou's expression hardened. He took Corey's hands and leaned in, looking him straight in the eye. "Listen to me, Corey, and let this sink in. Now that you have experienced this, you will want to do it again. And again. You will become obsessed. You'll convince yourself that you are the chosen one, the only human who can change time. Take my word. Resist this. It has consequences. It will destroy you mentally. And physically."

Papou raised his hands upward. His fingers were gnarled and thick, covered with coarse hair like some prehistoric creature.

Corey flinched. "Are you going to be okay?"

"Our sister organization in Vancouver is working on a cure. That's why I left for Canada, Corey." Papou lowered his hands. "You know the expression 'Nature abhors a vacuum'? Well, Nature abhors time travel, too.

It violates all kinds of physical laws. If you hop back to a point within your lifetime, you'll exist twice—different ages at the same time. Like two identical poles on a magnet trying to occupy the same space. To compensate, your genes . . . shift. It is a natural protective mechanism. The body changes. Some people can make hundreds of time hops just fine, some only once or twice—"

Before Papou could finish, a familiar voice cut through the night air. *"Corey, that was a really dumb prank!"*

Leila came bounding toward him, her Catwoman cape flowing in the breeze. Corey gave his papou a look. "I think I'm in trouble."

"This kind of trouble," Papou murmured, "you can handle."

"Oh, hey, Leila," Corey said, bolting to his feet. "Um, sorry, I got sidetracked."

"I have been looking all over for you! Do you know what I just saw, coming over here? The biggest rat in the history of New York City. With teeth the size of machetes. I could have rabies by now!" As Leila turned to the old man, her angry expression melted. "P-P-Papou? Is that you?"

"Hello, *koukla mou*—my dear girl," he said, opening his arms. "How are you and your mother?"

She practically leaped at Corey's grandfather, throwing her arms around him. Her bad mood was completely forgotten. "I am soooo happy to see you!"

"It is not every day an old man is hugged by Catwoman," Papou said. "I forgot it is Halloween! Do you two have a party over at GWC?"

"GWC?" Leila said.

"Your school, silly one," Papou replied. "George Washington Carver Middle School!"

Leila laughed. "No, silly. That's where *you* went, maybe. We go to FPR."

She pointed to a glass-and-steel tower that rose just peeking over the trees north of One Hundredth Street on Central Park West.

"What the—when was *that* built?" Corey asked. "How did I miss that?"

"Very funny," Leila said.

Corey exchanged a baffled glance with his grandfather.

"Pardon me, dear?" Papou said. "But . . . FPR?"

Leila smiled. "Frederick P. Ruggles Middle School," she said.

"R-R-Ruggles . . . ?" Papou said.

Leila raised an eyebrow and sang to some vaguely familiar tune, "'All hail to fair Ruggles / Where despite all our struggles / We let inner strength be our guide! / Like our founder whose bravery / Fought a war against slavery / We're the pride of the Upper West Side.'"

The words hung in the misty air. Corey felt light-headed. He thought back to the gunshot. The black smoke.

"Corey, what exactly happened between you and that soldier?" Papou murmured.

"Wait—*soldier?*" Leila said.

"Ruggles," Corey said. "That was his name—Ruggles! He was going to shoot himself. But I distracted him."

He turned to meet Papou's eyes, which were the size of baseballs. "He should have died . . . ," the old man said, his voice tight and raspy. "But because of you, he lived. 'Fought a war against slavery' . . . he fought for the North. A hero."

"Um, unlike you, I hate codes," Leila said. "Would you mind translating?"

But neither Corey nor Papou had the words to express what was in their minds.

In the annals of New York history before Corey's trip, Ruggles had become a corpse in Central Park that day.

Until he met Corey.

And then he wasn't.

9

Smig, once known as Cosmo deSmiglia, had not been dealt a favorable hand by life. Scaring people wasn't fun. Nor was the constant snuffling, drooling, and farting that came with his predicament.

But his hearing and sight were better than ever. There were some advantages to the curse of time travel.

They called this transspeciating, a fancy name for transforming into an extinct species. This supposedly prevented you from duplicating any living thing when you time-hopped. But this was a cruel joke—a *stinked* species, it seemed to him.

That was funny. Smig snorted. But he hated the smell of his own breath.

He thought of all the other things he could have

become. Like a Neanderthal. Or a flying reptile. *Those* would have been fun.

Staying safely hidden behind the Glen Span Arch, he watched the trio on the park bench and the skyline behind them. He'd heard every word the old man and the girl had said. By rights he should have been furious. If there really was a cure, the timing was horrible. Way too late for him.

Also, the girl had called him a rat. He hated when people called him a rat.

Still, he couldn't keep his eyes from the sight across the street. The gleaming new high-rise silhouetted against the setting sun. A high-rise that had never, ever been there.

As one-time keeper of the Knickerbocker logs, Smig had read all the legends, the ancient tales of mythical people who could do the impossible. Who could change history and thus bend the course of present-day events.

They were called Throwbacks.

But these were myths, tall tales. Silly creatures conjured out of a need to explain something unexplainable. Like sprites in the woods who people claimed to see but never actually caught. No one ever took those stories seriously.

Now, Smig thought, *no one would ever not.*

He knew people who would like to learn about this. Powerful people. Maybe powerful enough to get this cure for themselves and restore him to the way he had been.

He heard a noise and looked up. The three were leaving now.

With a snuffle that could not be helped, Smig backed away, deeper into the woods.

10

Throwback.

Corey didn't like when Papou had used the term. It was the kind of thing teachers said—*You're such a throwback to some more civilized era, Corey.* It was right up there with *You have such a vivid imagination* in the list of Top Ten Things That Made Corey Cringe.

But Papou was using that word as a kind of official, technical term. It was the type of time traveler Corey had become. Someone who had the power to do things no one else could do.

As they emerged from the park at One Hundredth Street, Papou was telling Leila the truth about what had just happened. She had taken off her Catwoman mask, and her face was ashen.

"So that photo I found . . . ," she murmured. "That really was *you* in it, Corey. You were talking to the stonemason."

"When I hopped into the past, I was in your bathroom," Corey replied. "Which means I came out of someone else's bathroom in the 1800s. She was not pleased. I booked."

"So a few minutes later she looks out the window, spots you talking to the mason, and takes a photo—to identify you to the constables!" Papou said. "Of course, it would have taken her quite some time to produce the photo—sending the film to a laboratory and what have you. But that photo survived into the twenty-first century."

The trio stopped at Central Park West. The old man propped himself up on the lamppost, looking around hollow eyed. "The school isn't the only difference," he said.

"The street looks like it was paved," Corey said. "And the stone wall is so clean. No more soot. They weren't like that when I . . . hopped?"

Papou gestured toward the shops along the street. "Rainbow Brothers Supermarket . . . Faisal Cleaners . . . they weren't here either."

"I did that?" Corey shook his head. "Conjured a

supermarket? This is so cool. . . ."

Leila cocked her head. "Hello? No conjuring. Faisal has been there since before I was born. Rainbow, too."

Her words hung in the air for a moment. "I—wait—*what?*" Corey said.

"For. Ev. Ver," Leila said.

"That makes no sense," Corey insisted.

Papou's face grew dark. He gave Corey a pained look. "*Paithi mou,* what you have done is very, very serious."

In the silence, music blasted from the rooftop gym of the Frederick P. Ruggles Middle School across the street. Corey stared. It was freaky to see a building that had never existed before, in a neighborhood he knew like the back of his hand.

It was even freakier when Claudia Ramos ran up to him out of nowhere and planted a wet kiss on his left cheek. "Heyyy, Cee Fletch," she sang, whipping her Wonder Woman cape across her face. "See you inside."

"Gahhhh!" Corey said, wiping his cheek in disgust.

As Claudia skipped across the street, Leila scowled at Corey. "Why'd you react like that?"

"*Cee Fletch?*" Corey repeated. "No one has ever *ever* called me that!"

"Uh, it's been your nickname forever," Leila said.

"Corey Powder, Nerd on a Stick, Fletcher in the

Rye—*those* are my nicknames," Corey said. "But not Cee Fletch. And the last time I saw Claudia Ramos she said she wished I were a tweet, so she could delete me. She has hated my guts since we were in diapers."

"You went out with her all last year," Leila insisted.

"*Nooooo!*" Corey put his head in his hands and sank next to Leila on the park bench. "Is this what I've done? I save a guy's life, and now I'm forced to *like* Claudia Ramos?"

"Corey, do you remember the Ray Bradbury story I read to you as a boy?" Papou asked.

"'A Sound of Thunder' . . ." Corey nodded. "It was about the butterfly effect. Where a group goes into the prehistoric past, one of them steps on a butterfly, and when they get back, the world is at the brink of nuclear war."

"I cannot stress enough, Corey, you must never—"

"But that was just a *story*," Corey pleaded. "I know what you're going to tell me. I can't time-hop ever again. But I did, and nothing bad happened. I saved someone's life and improved the neighborhood!"

"What if Ruggles had shot you?" Papou said. "What if he went on to have a child who was a serial killer? Or bought a Model T and ran someone over?"

"That's so morbid," Leila said.

"When you can change the past, all bets are off!" Papou replied. "The probability for bad things to happen is astronomical. Look at me, *paithi mou*—you can't do this. For many reasons. What happens when the word gets out among the time-hopping community? Do you think they're all granola-eating peace-loving nerds? There are shadow factions, cult groups who have spent ages trying to prove that Throwbacks actually exist, that they're not like unicorns or griffins. If they find you, they will use you. To try to change history for their own evil motives. Corey, this is way too important to shrug off."

"What am I supposed to do?" Corey asked.

"I'm afraid you will need to . . . disappear," Papou replied.

"Like, die?" Leila said.

Papou tented his fingers on his forehead. "No, *disappear*. To an undisclosed location. With a new identity. I see no other way out of this. These people will kidnap you in the blink of an eye, Corey."

"What about Mom, Dad, Zenobia . . . *you?*" Corey pleaded. "Who will I live with?"

"I have friends all over the world. They will help." Papou stood.

"What about Leila?" Corey said. "Her aunt was in

that book club that wasn't really a book club."

"The Knickerbockers, yes," Papou said.

"So she was a time-hopper." Corey spun to look at Leila. *"You're a blood relation.* Maybe you can time travel, too!"

"I doubt it. I'm not like you, Corey. I have no imagination. I'm too normal," Leila said.

"So I'll do it myself." Corey's mind was churning. "Traveling in time, changing things—that means actually being able to make right the things that should never have happened. How can that be bad?"

Papou shook his head. "Corey, no."

"Saving Ruggles's life was good a thousand ways," Corey insisted. "Think of the other lives I could save, Papou."

"You're scaring me, *paithaki*," Papou said.

"Wait—nine-eleven did happen, didn't it?" Corey asked Leila. "Saving Ruggles didn't stop that?"

Papou muttered something in Greek as he yanked the phone from his pocket. He furiously began tapping away, an expectant look on his face. Corey looked over his shoulder. The screen filled with a list from a website of victims from the 9/11 attack—and there, in alphabetical order, was the name Maria Fletcher.

The old man's shoulders sank. "It did happen."

"I could have told you that," Leila said softly.

"Leila, I can do what Papou couldn't," Corey replied. "I can save my grandmother. Was it fair that Papou had to go through the torture of watching her die three times?"

Papou bowed his head. "Four . . ."

"I'm a Throwback," Corey said. "And you're someone who was cheated out of a happy life by some maniacs in 2001."

"This is crazy, Corey," Leila said. "What if you don't survive?"

"I can't die before I was born," Corey pointed out. "That's impossible."

"Did you seriously just say that?" Leila asked. "In the life of Corey, impossible is the new possible."

"We all know when the planes hit. We know the exact moment. Which means I'll know exactly when it's time to run away." Corey turned to his grandfather. "When Zenobia and I were little, I remember staying at your apartment, Papou. Mom and Dad warned us not to be scared if you talked in your sleep. But it wasn't just talking. We could hear you through the closed door. You screamed and moaned. You called her name. It seemed to last for hours. Zenobia held on to me the whole time, and we both cried. We felt so bad for you."

A tear broke loose from Papou's eyelid and made its way down his cheek. "I—I didn't know that."

"You were there for me today, Papou. You've always been there for me. Now I want to do what's right for you." He kneeled next to his grandfather and put a hand on his bony shoulder. "I'm scared. I didn't ask for any of this. If you think moving away and getting a new identity is the right thing to do, then say the word, and I'm down for it. But tell me, if you were a Throwback, what would *you* do? Would you try to save her?"

Papou's breathing was loud and shallow. He stared at the ground for a long time, saying nothing. Across the street, people shouted Leila's and Corey's names, but neither of them responded.

"We don't have to tell Mom and Dad about this trip," Corey said softly. "We don't even have to let them know you're back until it's over. It will be quick. Just between us. Or between us and . . . *Yiayia*. Because you may never have to lose her."

At the sound of the Greek word for *grandmother*, Papou shivered. When he finally spoke, his voice was papery and thin: "All right, then. You'll need an artifact."

Corey nearly screamed. "Really? You mean it?"

"You can't be serious!" Leila shouted in dismay.

"*Stamati*, both of you," Papou snapped. "Be quiet.

My trips to 2001 required a subway token minted in that year. You will find it in my safe, in the room where I used to live. The combination is your birthday and Zenobia's, July twenty-fifth and February sixth—seven, twenty-five, two, six. I also have notes in there about your grandmother. I knew her routine cold. But on that day, I believe she got off at a different train station. Or went to work early. I can't know for sure. You see, we were occupying different apartments then. Separated, you would say."

"Really?" Corey said. "You never told me."

"It's not a conversation I enjoy," Papou replied. "Now, getting to the right time and place is not easy. You may be off by a day or a week. It took me a few times to get the hang of it. The past moments are all there, stacked within our present consciousness. Your brain has to focus on the right one. Like I said, meta-physical and physical. But the time of day will remain the same—you go now, at five, you arrive in the past at five. So to get there in the morning, you must wait until the morning."

"No, Corey," Leila said. "No, no, and no. This is too dangerous. I know it's your wife . . . your grandmother. I mean, it's so important, I get that. But what did you just say about time travel—all bets are off, right? Saving

Ruggles *could* have gone badly. What if this does, too?"

Papou took her black-gloved hand in his. "Leila, this isn't only about my wife. I'm thinking about Corey, too. Things have changed for him. He faces danger now, in the present, for who he is. People will be coming after him. He is safer in the past. And if he does change things . . . well, the year 2001 is so much more recent than the Civil War era. The changes aren't likely to be that great."

"Really?" Leila asked. "Or is that wishful thinking?"

Papou looked away. But Leila didn't let go of his hand.

"But, yeah . . . ," she said. "I do get it. And you can trust me to secrecy."

"Is that a yes?" Corey said.

Leila nodded. "I guess."

"Brava, Catwoman." Papou quietly turned to Corey, his eyes filling with tears. "Go now, *paithi mou*. Before I change my mind."

11

Carefully Corey pushed open the door to his grand-father's bedroom. A classic Papou smell wafted out, sweet and musty. Corey realized the room hadn't been aired for a long time. Against the far wall was a single bed with a down blanket. The walls were lined with books. Near the front window was a rolltop desk with a stack of newspapers.

He didn't know the room well. Never had. It was always Papou's private place. On top of the desk was an empty silver frame. The photo had somehow slipped out of the bottom of the frame and slid onto a pile of papers. Corey flipped it over. What he saw made him grin. In it, Papou was young and dark haired, with a thick mustache and a Greek fisherman's cap. He was on a sailboat, bare chested and tan, with his arm around a gorgeous young woman with a freckled nose. They both looked as if the photographer had caught them in the middle of a joke.

Corey flipped the photo over and read the blue fountain pen scrawl across the back:

Gus + Maria HONEYMOON
@ LOS CABOS, MEXICO!!!

He'd never seen a photo of his grandmother so young. He tried to slip it back into the slot out of which it had fallen, but the halves of the silver frame separated and fell apart. Something metallic slipped out, tumbling onto the floor.

A key.

Corey scooped it up and put it on the desk. It wasn't going to do him much good. Papou had given him numbers for a combination lock.

Through the door, he could hear his mom talking on the phone in the kitchen. She didn't know he was in here, and he didn't want to have to explain. Quietly, quickly Corey checked around the room for the safe. He had forgotten to ask Papou what it looked like, how big it was. Under the bed he found only slippers and dust bunnies. The dresser drawers contained nothing but clothing. He searched through the papers on the desk and in a file cabinet, then checked behind every piece of framed artwork on the walls. No safe.

Eyeballing the floor for any signs of secret trapdoors, he moved slowly to Papou's closet. The knob would not move. He yanked on the door anyway, but it was locked tight.

Under the knob was an old-fashioned keyhole.

"Corey!" his mom called from the kitchen. "Can you be ready in fifteen?"

Corey edged to the door, slipped it open, and peeked into the hallway. "Sure, Mom!"

He ducked back in and shut the door. Turning back to the desk, he grabbed the key and shoved it into the closet door keyhole.

It turned easily. With a soft click, the door opened. An automatic light went on inside. The closet was deep, with racks full of hanging clothes on the left and right. On the back wall was a huge framed map of the New York City subway system.

Corey pushed the map to the left. It swung on its hook, revealing a small rectangular door with a combination lock and a handle.

Perfect.

The combination is your birthday and Zenobia's, Papou had said. 7-25-2-6.

Spinning the dial, he stopped carefully at each number, then pushed down the handle. With a deep click, the door swung open to reveal a small cube padded with gray carpeting. It contained a plastic bag, a small manila envelope, and a spiral notebook.

Corey removed it all and stuffed it into his backpack. He slammed the safe door shut and scooted back to his own room. There, he pulled out the plastic bag and held it up to the lamplight. Inside was a gold-colored coin the size of a quarter but not as heavy. The letters NYC were stamped on it. He took it out, felt it grow warm in his hand, then placed it gently on the desk.

He shivered.

This was his artifact. His portal. The token that would take him to a place no one in his right mind would want to be.

Next he looked at the spiral notebook. On the front, in Papou's handwriting, were the words MARIA HARVOULAKIS FLETCHER, 9/11/01. His grandmother's name. Papou's notes. His attempts at rescue. The pages were graph paper, every inch crammed with handwritten comments and cutout newspaper articles.

Quickly Corey phoned Papou. "So, I have the token. Also your notebook. There's a manila envelope, too, but I haven't opened it."

"Manila envelope?" Papou said. "I've forgotten what's inside that."

Corey opened it and pulled out a small, worn-out blue booklet. "Looks like a passport," he said, flipping to the first page. "Dated 1917. Some guy named . . . something Greeky. I can't pronounce it."

"Ah, yes—that would be Evanthis Harvoulakis," Papou said. "He's your great-great-grandfather, on your grandmother's side."

"Easy for you to say."

"*Evanthis*—like the name *Yvonne*, and the first part of the word *thesis*. Rhymes with fleece."

"Yvonne Theece," Corey said. "Evanthis."

"Your grandmother adored him. She loved to take me to Ellis Island, where he came in as an immigrant. We would go to the address where he grew up, the downtown corner where he ran a fruit stand. Both places are gone now, but she has old photos. We would take them with us and try to match them to the location. Funny, I'm the time traveler, but your grandmother—she really felt a connection to the past." Papou sighed. "Anyway, *paithaki*, read my notes if you can. I know you never met her, but sometimes a fresh eye is good. At least you'll get a sense of what she was like. If you can gain any clues to where she went that morning, bravo to you. I wrote out her usual schedule, but I'm not sure it will help."

"So she wasn't in your apartment that morning?" Corey asked. "You two were . . . ?"

"We were fighting, Corey," Papou said. "I can't even remember why. She was no longer living there with me. I don't know where she was that morning. Probably with some friend—but she had hundreds of friends. Don't stay up too late with the notes. Leave the house around six fifteen. The trains will be empty. Take the C to Fulton. Don't forget the token."

"What do I do when I get there?" Corey asked. "Just squeeze the token and think of nine-eleven?"

Papou sighed. "It's not an exact science. But it helps to know where you want to go. In the spiral notebook I think there's a photo of your grandmother near one of the towers. Take that, too. If you can, go to the same spot as the photo. Block out everything else. Don't be nervous. It doesn't work if you're too nervous. And clutch tightly to that token. Do you need me to come with you? I can, you know. But I won't be much good.

Unfortunately, this will work best if you do it alone."

"Yeah," said Corey uncertainly. "Okay."

"If you don't get it right, come home. Be sure you have some change in your pocket from now. Metal! Coins! You can always try again another time."

"I'll be all right." Corey smiled. "Hey. I bet she's awesome."

"The fig doesn't fall far from the tree," Papou said.

"You mean apple," Corey corrected him.

"I mean fig. There are no apples in Greece." Papou chuckled. When he spoke again, his voice was thicker and softer. "I love you, Corey. I will be praying. Stay safe."

Corey's eyes blinked open at 4:15 a.m.

It was too quiet. He needed the rumble of traffic on Ninety-Fifth Street. The world felt fake without it.

Sliding out of bed, he went to the desk and turned on his lamp. Papou's notebook stood open. He flipped through the pages and tried to make sense of it.

Most of it was lists: INTERESTS, HOBBIES, FAVOR-ITE RESTAURANTS, CONTACTS, MEMBERSHIPS. There were lots of photos of her, from her childhood all the way up to 2001. Pictures of their honeymoon in Mexico. A photo of her doing a crazy exaggerated ballet pose in front of one of the World Trade Towers.

That last one was the photo Papou wanted him to take. As Corey set it aside, he smiled at the image. She looked taller than Papou. Her hair was thick, dark, and tightly pulled back. In other images, when she let her hair down, it exploded outward like a storm cloud. She had an intense, no-nonsense look but also a huge grin. The last photo was dated August 2001. Her hair was half-gray. She and Papou were with friends in a restaurant, and neither of them looked happy.

That was the last one. After the photos was a section marked DOWNLOADS, where Papou had pasted some printouts from websites. Corey unfolded the first one and read the header:

SAINT NICHOLAS
GREEK ORTHODOX CHURCH

155 Cedar Street, New York, NY (original address) Erected 1832, consecrated as a church 1922, destroyed 2001 in World Trade Tower collapse, rebuilt as a National Shrine.

LIST OF ORIGINAL FOUNDERS

Corey scanned the founders list, which was full of unpronounceable Greek names. But Papou had circled one:

**E. HARVOULAKIS,
127 LIBERTY STREET**

So old Evanthis—his grandmother's grandfather—had been one of the people who established the church. That was cool. *Your grandmother adored him,* Papou had said. *We would go to the address where he grew up, the downtown corner where he ran a fruit stand.*

At this hour, Papou was asleep. Also, his phone was most likely off. But Corey sent him a text anyway:

> was her papou still alive in 2001?
> would she have gone to his place?
> or the spot where he lived?

> you said she liked to remember him.
> was there anything special about that day
> that had anything to do with him?
> a bday or something?
> it might be a clue to where she went . . .
> just saying . . .

He sent the message and glanced at the printout again. Across the bottom of the page was a footer:

JOIN OUR CONGREGATION!
SUNDAY WORSHIP • SUNDAY SCHOOL
BAPTISM • NAME DAY • FUNERAL SERVICES

Corey sat bolt upright. He thought about all the great parties he'd had as a kid—parties that made Leila and his other friends jealous. For the Greeks, name days were more important than birthdays. Like February 10, which was the big celebration for anyone with the name Charalambos—which was Corey's official Greek first name.

What about Evanthis?

Corey quickly did a search on "Evanthis Name Day." Right away he found a list of Greek Name Days that was enormous, over multiple pages. He clicked on "E" and scrolled down.

When he found what he needed, he had to take a deep, deep breath.

EVANTHIS..................SEPTEMBER 11

12

I am entering stegosaurus.
btw, I think I know where
she might have gone.
<3 u!!!

As he left the C train at the Fulton Street subway station, Corey sent the text to Papou. The old man would know what it meant.

If you had to go back in time, this seemed like the right place to start. The station was called the Oculus and looked like some kind of movie superhero lair. Its floor was the size of a football field, with walls of curved white metal crossbeams that arched upward like giant ribs. At the top the ribs met at a thin glass ceiling, like a spine. When he first saw this as a little kid, he felt like he'd been swallowed up by a stegosaurus.

Corey rode the escalator to an exit marked the National September 11 Memorial & Museum. Outside, a crowd had begun to form even though it wasn't even 7 a.m. The glass skyscrapers blazed in the morning sun. It was much hotter than usual for an early November morning and already he had broken a sweat. From the outside, the Oculus looked less like a dinosaur than a giant white hair clip. He reached into his pocket and pulled out the old photo of his grandmother in front of the World Trade tower. Her face was slightly blurry, her head thrown back in laughter, as if Papou had just told a joke.

If you can, go to the same spot as the photo, Papou had said. *Block out everything else. Don't be nervous. It doesn't work if you're too nervous. And clutch tightly to that token.*

How could he know what the "same spot" was? Everything from 2001 was gone—destroyed, and then rebuilt into something completely different looking. As he reached for his phone again, a tiny girl with curly red hair thrust a drippy rainbow-colored ice cream cone practically into his face.

Corey sprang back. *"Gaaah!"*

"You want this?" she asked. "I hate it."

"No!" Corey squeaked. "I mean, no thanks, I don't!"

The girl seemed offended. She stuck out her tongue and let the cone drop at his feet. He was vaguely aware of her mom pulling her away and apologizing.

Don't be nervous. It doesn't work if you're too nervous.

Corey took three deep cleansing breaths. He told himself to chill. Now he noticed a small crowd heading toward the black marble wall that surrounded one of the two giant reflecting pools. The pools were supposed to represent the footprints of the two towers. His grandmother had worked in one of the towers. So there was a logical place to start.

He made his way over, breathing in . . . breathing out. . . .

Just an ordinary day . . . traveling into the past, la-la-la . . . to the worst domestic attack in US history . . .

From around the pool's entire square perimeter, water cascaded gently down into the deep, shadowy pit. He tried not to think of what had been there. The mangled mass of offices, restaurants, bathrooms, computers, paper, water coolers, carpets, paintings, phones. Three thousand human beings, who had done nothing more than show up for work on a clear, gorgeous day.

Breathe in . . . breathe out . . .

Corey held up the photo and tried not to think of

all that. In the image's background, behind his grand-mother, were a couple of tan brick Art Deco buildings. Had they survived?

Yes. They were still there. Across the vast plaza, over the heads of the tourists. The same wall of windows looked down on the scene. As if nothing had ever hap-pened. He tried to tune out the crowd. He still wasn't sure how this worked. The only other times he'd time-hopped were accidents. He'd never tried to do it on purpose. Did you have to be in *exactly* the same place? Like, be in the footsteps of the photographer?

"Is that your mommy?"

The little girl, now without an ice cream cone, was staring up at his photo and pointing to his dead *yia-yia*'s smiling face. A few steps beyond, her parents were looking at their phones, arguing about how to get to the South Street Ferry.

"It's my grandma," Corey said. "But a long time ago."

"Is she dead?" the girl asked.

"How did you know?"

The girl shrugged. "People died here. My mom and dad knew somebody, too. That's why everybody comes. Can I see?" As Corey crouched to show her the photo, the girl smiled. "She's pretty."

"Was," Corey said.

"You can see her again, you know." The girl cast a quick glance toward her parents, then lowered her voice to a whisper. "When my doggy died? Fluffy? I cried so much. I took his picture to bed with me. I looked at it and looked at it and pretended he was alive. I told him how much I missed him. 'I miss you I miss you I miss you. . . .' I was holding his collar, too. It still smelled like him. And then . . ." She thrust out her arms as if to say *TA-DA!* "There he was! He licked me and everything! Then I had to come back."

Now she had Corey's attention. "Come back? From where?"

"From when he was alive, silly. I think it was like last June. 'Cause when I saw Fluffy, I saw me, too. I was in bed wearing Pete the Cat pj's. And I stopped liking Pete the Cat in June."

"Wait. You saw yourself in bed?" Corey said.

Before the girl could respond, her mom lunged toward her and took her hand. "I'm *soooo* so sorry!" she said to Corey with a nervous laugh. "Maddie likes to talk. She has *such* an active imagination. Let's say good-bye now, sweetie! Mommy and Daddy are going!"

Maddie heaved her shoulders wearily. But as she turned to go, she called back over her shoulder. "Remember, talk to her. Say how much you miss her!"

Corey waved back to her with his free hand. He was shaking.

Active imagination. Right.

She was like him. Did she understand?

How many were there?

Corey had to block it out. He had a job to do. He held up the photo again, using it as a guide, lining up the angle. Trying to guess where his grandmother had been standing. Wandering left and right.

From behind, someone banged into him. "Oh. Sorry," Corey said.

A man in a sleek suit sneered at him. "Tourist."

Corey ignored the comment. Wandering was not good when you were among New Yorkers, who liked to walk very fast in very straight lines. But you couldn't walk fast if you didn't know where to go. And now the voices were clamoring all around him:

"Excuse me. . . ."

"Whoa, traffic jam . . ."

"Keep it moving, bud. . . ."

"This isn't Iowa. . . ."

He blocked out the nastier remarks. He didn't care. All he saw right then was his grandmother's face. The kindness in her eyes leaped out of the photo.

Talk to her. Say how much you miss her. . . .

The little girl's words seemed silly, but he took a deep breath and said, "Hi. Um, yeah, so this is your grandson? Corey?"

A guy with slicked-back hair bumped into him from the left, nearly knocking the photo from his hand. "Dude, can you please move to the curb?"

A street sweeper was barreling down the block, brushing up clouds of dust in the gutter. Corey edged toward the curb, out of the flow of foot traffic but a few feet from the street sweeper's path. "Okay, I know this is ridiculous because you're just a photo," he continued, "and I never even met you. But I just wanted to say, I miss you. I know all about you and I miss you so much. But most of all . . . Papou misses you, too. Every day. More than anything in the world . . ."

His eyes were moist now. The throng of people became a blur, the voices fading to a murmur—until someone knocked into him from behind. Again.

The photo flew from his hand and drifted to the ground, where it landed in the gutter. The street sweeper was only a few feet away. He saw Corey and jammed on his brakes.

All Corey saw was the massive, filthy, rotating brush. And the image.

Her eyes.

He reached out to grab the photo. He felt the spray of water and debris on his back. Heard the raucous clang of a horn.

He scrambled for the curb and felt the pressure of bristles on his back. Pulling him down, taking him to the street. Behind him someone shrieked.

And everything went white.

13

He woke up screaming.

Leaning over him was a guy with thick glasses. He was wearing a blue jacket, baggy pleated pants, and a lanyard with a plastic ID card labeled "Clifton Swank." "Hey, yo, kid," he said in a thick New York accent. "You okay?"

Corey sat bolt upright. The sweeper was gone. It had missed him. It had missed a lot of garbage, too. Pages of newspapers were swirling in the air like dancing ghosts. He breathed in a gulp of air and shivered.

"It got cooler," Corey said. "How long was I unconscious?"

"I don't know, I just got here," Swank said. "I can't believe people just left you in the gutter. Welcome to

New York, huh? Your parents around?"

"No," Corey said, rubbing his eyes.

"Sit still, my friend. Let me call nine-one-one. . . ."

Before Corey could reply, a sheet of newspaper whapped him in the face. As he peeled it off, he couldn't help noticing the headline:

PARENTS INCREASINGLY ALLOW HIGH SCHOOL CHILDREN TO OWN MOBILE TELEPHONES, CITING SAFETY CONCERNS

"What the——?" His eyes darted to the top of the page.

NEW YORK DAILY NEWS
SEPTEMBER 11, 2001

Corey's blood was pumping so hard he thought his heart would spring right out of his mouth and splat into the street. "So . . ." He had to gulp to keep from choking. "It's . . . it's nine-eleven?"

"Nine-one-one, three digits that save lives!" Clifton Swank was punching buttons on a flip phone the size of a shoe. "The medics will take care of you."

Over Swank's head loomed a steel-and-glass tower.

Its sides formed a perfect square, sheathed with vertical bands of steel, rising perfectly straight—no setback, no extra design. It was as if Jack's beans, instead of sprouting a stalk, had somehow caused a giant metal cage to stretch upward into the clouds.

"I. Don't. Believe this . . ." Corey glanced back toward the Oculus, but it was gone. So was the Memorial. In its place was a windswept cement plaza. And across the plaza was the other tower, absolutely identical, bouncing the sunlight into Corey's eyes.

He was there.

He'd made it.

Shielding his brow, he rose slowly. He had looked at a million images of the towers, but actually seeing them made him feel dizzy. It wasn't their beauty, exactly. They were plain and a little dull looking. But they stood like trees in a vast field, and that's what made them different from anything in the city. They weren't wedged into a thicket of buildings and narrow streets, like every other skyscraper. You saw them head to toe. It made them seem taller. Impossibly tall. Proud. Pure.

And they were about to disappear forever.

Corey sprang to his feet and looked at his phone. 8:03.

"Heyyyy, nice device . . . ," Swank said, looking away from his phone to stare at Corey's.

"Uh, I have to go," Corey said, shoving the phone into his pocket. "Do you know where 155 Cedar Street is?"

"Head down Washington Street, turn . . . left, I think? . . . on Cedar. That way." Swank pointed downtown. "Seriously, though, kid, you're not going anywhere just yet. We have a few minutes before the EMTs get here. So while we're waiting . . . y'know, I'm involved in a tech startup. I'd love to see that mobile phone—"

"*My phone?*" Corey whirled to face the guy.

"Whoa . . . dude . . . ," Swank said, backing away. "Touchy . . ."

"Okay, sorry. Didn't mean to yell. But listen to me, and listen close. Promise me you won't think I'm crazy?"

Swank shrugged. "Sure."

"Forget about my phone. And forget about the EMTs. They will be having a long day. Go home—now! Call everyone you know who works down here, and tell them to go home, too. In forty minutes, three thousand people are going to die."

"Wait, *what?*" Swank said.

"The first plane hits at eight forty-six, the second at nine oh three. By the end of the day the Twin Towers are gone. Do you understand—*gone*. As in, piles of smoking steel."

"Uh-huh. Right." Swank held up his hand and made a V sign. "How many fingers do you see?"

"Just listen to me—we don't have time!"

By now, two other strangers had stopped to listen. Corey turned away and sprinted across the plaza. He could hear Swank calling out behind him.

An ambulance was making its way up Church Street. It was probably the one Swank had called for him. Corey ducked behind a mail truck parked at the curb. Quickly he unfolded a sheet he'd taken from Papou's notebook.

MARIA FLETCHER 9/11/01 SCHEDULE

5:45 a.m. Probable wake-up time. Would not tell me who she stayed with. Most likely Amy on Prospect Park West, Sarah on East 73rd, Lauren on Bethune St. She liked to go for a morning run before leaving for work.

8:07 a.m. Normal time she emerged from C train at Fulton Street Station (Fulton and Broadway). Walked west on Fulton toward World Trade Center. Could not find her. Possibly took other train besides C.

8:07–8:30 a.m. Coffee, newspaper, etc. I searched for her in every coffee shop from Cedar to Duane and from Washington to Broadway. Still leaves plenty more!

8:30 a.m. Approximate arrival at office at Karelian Group, 95th floor, Tower 2.

Corey focused on the 8:07–8:30 part. That was the big unknown. Just because his *yiayia* usually went to a coffee shop didn't mean she always did.

It was time for Corey to test his hunch. He had a feeling about where she'd gone this morning.

Reaching into his backpack, he pulled out the yellowed passport of his great-great-grandfather. "I can't pronounce your name," he whispered, staring into the grim, thickly mustached face, "but happy name day anyway. And if you're in a place where you can look down on this day, please help me out. Please."

People were now thronging out of the subway stop a block away, filling the plaza. Corey peered around the corner of the truck. The ambulance was stopped where he had been a few moments ago. He couldn't see Clifton Swank through the crowd.

Good.

Clutching the passport and the photo of his grand-mother, Corey sprinted south across the plaza. "*Go home!*" he shouted, dodging commuters left and right. "*Everybody, go home!*"

No one stopped. A few people looked at him like he was crazy. This was useless. As he reached the edge of the plaza, he saw a sign for Washington Street, heading south. He barreled across the street, narrowly missing being hit by a biker and two taxis. Washington Street was narrow and dark, and as he took a left on Cedar, he checked the address.

Instead of a churchy-looking building, 155 Cedar was a simple brownstone, actually brown. A bulletin board in a glass case announced ST. NICHOLAS GREEK ORTHODOX CHURCH with a long list of future events—events Corey knew would never occur. He climbed the stoop and pulled open a glass door.

The entry foyer looked like any other Greek church—a Christ icon on a table in the center, a wooden table with square wooden cubbies for different-sized candles and donations, another table containing a sand pit to insert the lit candles. Behind the foyer was a church that stretched to the back of the building, with dark wooden pews.

A silver-haired man, wearing a navy-blue suit, was

picking up papers from the pews. "May I help you, young man?" he said in a thick Greek accent.

"I'm looking for Maria Fletcher?" Corey said.

The man knitted his eyebrows. "I don't know the name."

"She looks like this." Corey ran to him, holding out the photo of her, now stained from the fall into the gutter. "Her grandfather's name was . . ." He took a deep breath and tried to remember the pronunciation. "Yvonne . . . theese. *Evanthis*."

"Ah, today is his name day," the man said.

"Yes!" Corey's pulse raced. "Yes, that's exactly right! So I thought . . . maybe she might be here. Do people come to the church on name days?"

The man shrugged. "Some do, yes. Would you like to sit and wait?"

Corey checked his watch. 8:13.

If he was right, she would show up any minute. If he was wrong, she was on her way to work.

"I have to check something," he said, pulling his phone from his pocket. "If she comes in, tell her to stay, okay? What's your cell number?"

The man laughed. "This is a church, not a prison. There are no cells."

"Cell *phone!*" Corey said, grabbing a flyer from a

table. "Here. I'll write my phone number on this. Please text me if she comes."

"Text?"

"*Call!*"

"I'm Taso, and here's my card, if you need to call me," the man said, reaching into his pocket for a business card. "If she arrives, whom shall I say is asking?"

Corey almost said *her grandson*. But she didn't have a grandson in 2001. "Her husband. I mean, *I'm* not her husband. I . . . work for him. This is important."

He raced out of the church, back the way he came. He examined the face of every person on the sidewalk. He ducked into a coffee shop, a Mexican restaurant, and a burger place, making sure to check every newsstand. As he emerged onto the plaza again, he checked the time. 8:21.

On the plaza, people were crisscrossing every which way. They walked faster than people in the present. It took Corey a moment to realize why. No one was looking down at a phone. Which made it easier to see faces.

"*Maria Fletcher!*" Corey didn't care if he sounded like a nutcase. "*Maria!*"

A cabdriver, stopped at a light, hung his head out the driver window, and sang the "Maria" song from *West Side Story*.

"Not funny!" Corey snapped.

"You looking for somebody?" he said.

Corey held out the photo. "My grandmother. It's an emergency! A big one."

"Import-export, right?" the guy said, nodding. "The Karelian Group?"

Corey nearly dropped the photo. "Wait, you know her?"

"Nahhh, but I seen the face. This is my beat. The workers tip good, so I hang here every morning. That gang—the Karelian people? A lot of 'em do the Cosmic Diner for breakfast. Can't guarantee, but we could check it out."

Corey jumped into the cab. The driver's ID plate said his name was Eddie. Eddie did a U-turn, leaning on the horn. He sped west on Liberty Street and took a sharp turn on Church. As he wove in and out of traffic, Corey checked his call log.

The last message was from Leila. From the future. From the network account his parents paid for. Many, many years from now.

Would that even work now?

Quickly he pulled out Taso's business card and tapped out the number.

Nothing.

"Head back!" Corey said. "To the Greek church."

"But we—"

"Now! St. Nicholas's. Do you know where it is?"

Eddie yanked the steering wheel to the left. "Fasten that belt, kid. I own these streets!"

14

Corey wished he could time travel through red lights. In New York City they felt like eternities. Corey was racing up the steps of the Saint Nicholas Greek Orthodox Church only moments after he'd left, but it felt like it had been hours. Behind him, Eddie the cabdriver shouted, "Good luck!"

It was 8:31.

Taso was standing at the bottom of the stoop. "I attempted to phone you," he said softly. "Mrs. Vlechos arrived shortly after you left. But she told me she did not know you—"

"Thanks!" Corey blurted, barging through the front door.

"But—young man—" Taso sputtered.

Vlechos. That was the family name before it was changed to Fletcher. Corey raced through the front foyer, where a single slim, lit white candle stood in the sand pit near the icon. He stepped into the church. It was eerily quiet. A woman sat hunched at the end of a pew to his right. She was wearing a windbreaker, her head covered with a faded scarf. "Maria!" he shouted.

As he ran around the line of pews, he could barely breathe. What was he supposed to say? How did someone approach a grandmother he never knew? "Listen, I know you're not going to believe this . . . ," he began.

She looked up slowly. Beneath the scarf, her eyes were watery and gray, her face wrinkled. She gave him a bewildered smile.

Corey sprang back. "You're not Maria, are you?"

"Martha," she said.

"My boy, she's not here!" Taso's voice called out behind him.

Corey spun around to see the gray-haired man walking down the aisle. "Where is she?" Corey blurted. "You said she came here! You said you'd keep her—"

"I couldn't physically restrain her, my child. When I mentioned what you'd said, she grew agitated. She said she needed to get to work. She couldn't have gotten far." Taso turned and pointed to the right. "You may catch up to her if you hurry."

The words spilled out of Corey's mouth so fast they sounded like another language. "Please, when I go, clear the church. You leave, too. Go uptown while you can. Something very bad is going to happen. I can't explain. Just shut down and go. I know you think I'm crazy, but trust me!"

He couldn't wait for an answer. It was a church, so he said a silent prayer as he ran outside, jumped down the steps, and headed right toward Washington Street. She would be walking to the tower. There was only one route. He turned right again, north toward the wide plaza.

8:36.

The planes were in the air, on the way from Boston. The terrorists were in the pilots' seats. People had already died. Corey felt a wave of nausea.

There.

She was waiting for the light on Liberty Street.

He had never seen her in his life, but he knew. The hair matched the photos he had seen. Something about the posture, too. She was nearly as tall as he was, slender and dressed in elegant brown shoes, a gray skirt, and a light waist-length jacket.

"*Mariaaaaa!*"

She turned, looking around curiously. This time there were no surprises, no mistaken identity. The face was hers. But the sidewalk was narrow and jammed with people. She wasn't seeing Corey through the crowd.

Corey leaped off the curb and into the street, where the path would be faster. *"Over here!"*

The blare of a horn blotted out his cry. Behind him, tires screeched. Corey whirled around. A yellow cab bore down on him, trying to swerve out of the way. Its fender clipped him behind the knee, and Corey felt himself rising into the air. He thudded down on the cab's hood and rolled off, back onto the street.

He landed hard. For a moment he saw black. He leaped to his feet, gasping for air. People were already gathering around. The impact had made him let go of the passport and schedule, and he reached to scoop them up.

But another hand grabbed them first. "Are you all right?" a voice asked.

Surrounded by a growing crowd, standing tall and square-shouldered, was Maria Fletcher.

He grabbed her arm. He couldn't help himself. Her wrist was warm.

15

"You . . ." Corey spluttered. "I . . ."

She smiled. "It's okay," she said, her voice soft and soothing.

Yes. Yes, she was right, Corey thought. Everything was okay now.

He'd done it. He'd found her!

"You . . . ," Corey blurted out. "You're my *yiayia*."

Maria Fletcher shook him off and gave an odd smile, dusting off the passport. "No, I'm afraid I'm not. . . ."

"Okay. I—I know this is impossible to believe," he said, "but you cannot go to work today. We have to leave. You and me. I'll show you where to go."

She wasn't listening. She was staring at the photo inside the passport. "Um, where did you get this?"

Her smile was gone now. She looked at Corey with a mix of curiosity and bafflement.

"Papou gave it to me," Corey said. "Your husband. Gus Fletcher. Listen, I can explain—"

"Gus gave you my grandfather's passport?" she shot back. "Why?"

Corey froze. "That's . . . that's harder to answer than you think."

"And what's this?" She was scanning the schedule Papou had given him. "That's my routine. Are you some kind of intern for a private investigator? What's going on here? How old are you?"

Corey reached for her wrist. "Just . . . just come with me, okay? It's a long story. Please!"

She pulled away, shoving the passport and the schedule back to Corey. "Just . . . return these back to him," she said, backing away. "Honestly. Tell him I need my space. This is not helping—"

"You're going to die!" Corey blurted.

Now a New York City cop was approaching from the left. "Uh, excuse me, are you the kid who was hit by the vehicle?"

"It's okay!" Corey replied, turning to face the cop. "Just a light tap. I'm fine."

When he turned back, his grandmother was gone.

"Wait!" Corey shouted, taking off toward Liberty Street. She was halfway across as Corey approached the corner. But before he could reach it, a man in a hooded rain slicker leaped in his way. Corey slipped and steadied himself against a streetlight. "Stop her!" he shouted.

Now the light was red. The man in the slicker was dodging traffic, which was now fast, thick, and suicidal. Corey stood helplessly, watching as the man approached his grandmother from behind, tapping her on the shoulder.

For a moment Corey had a flicker of hope. Maybe the guy had heard him calling his grandmother. Maybe he was going to point her back to Corey. That would at least give him a chance to catch up.

But his hope curdled quickly. Maria was staring directly at the man. Her eyes widened and she backed away, her hand rising to cover her mouth. They were both in profile to him now. And Corey knew exactly who the man was. The only person who would be wearing a hooded raincoat on a clear day like this. A person who did not want to be seen until he was good and ready.

Papou.

His jaw dropped. This was not the Papou of 2001. This Papou was gray bearded and thin, looking not a moment younger than when Corey had last seen him.

I went many times to 2001 . . . , Papou had said, *to the day we lost your yiayia . . . I failed again and again.*

This was one of those times. Right here and now. This was one of Papou's time hops. Maria was staring into the face of her husband many years older. And it was freaking her out. Of course.

Corey jumped up and down, waving his arms over the blur of traffic. *"Listen to him! He's trying to save you!"* But his voice was lost in the noise.

He watched helplessly as Papou grabbed her arm, but she screamed. Right away a guy in a suit stepped between them, a stranger. Thinking he was a Good Samaritan, he pushed Papou away. Maria turned, running toward the Trade Center.

As the light turned green, Corey sprinted. Papou and Good Samaritan were in a screaming match. His grandmother was disappearing into the crowd. Corey picked up speed.

"Excuse me . . . excuse me. . . ." He pushed his way through the throng of workers, but he could no longer see her.

He had lost her.

Pivoting, he headed toward the One World Trade Center entrance. If he hurried, he could get there first, head her off before she entered the building. He wove through the rushing people like a linebacker. Moments ago, when Corey was in the present, people were grousing at him for being in the way. Now he was mad at them for the same reason.

Mad? How could he be mad? They were going to die!

He squeezed by people who were talking about stock prices. Boyfriends. Shoe sizes. A concert. As if these were the only important things in the world. "Excuse me . . . sorry . . . beep-beep," he chirped.

"Easy, pal, the sky ain't fallin'," a guy grumbled.

Corey spun around, but the man who said that was already by him, heading for the revolving doors for One World Trade Center. People lined up to enter. They were bored and sleepy and annoyed. They were chatting and checking their watches and phones, thinking about the day ahead. There was no throbbing music, no sense of dread, no warning. Corey wished he had more than a Throwback's skill. He wished he could stop time completely, stop the people cold, so he could take them away from here one by one to the river for safety. He would do that if he could, every one of them, inside the building and out. He would pull away three thousand people in that frozen instant, until the plaza was empty and the building was empty, and when time started again, the madmen would see all the emptiness and change their minds. . . .

There.

As he stood at the entrance, facing away from the building and into the crowd, he saw her.

She was hurrying toward the doors. Toward him. But before he could say a thing, someone else ran in front of her. Again.

This time it was a man in a winter parka, holding his arms wide as if he wanted to hug her. His grandmother stopped in her tracks and screamed. "Gus? What is going on here?"

No. No, no, no, no, no.

This was Papou, too. Without a beard. From a different time hop. From a longer time ago, when he was younger. "*I can explain!*" Corey shouted, running her way.

But his grandmother wasn't hearing him. She was bone white, as if she'd found herself in the middle of a nightmare. She turned away from Papou, pushing her way through a revolving glass door. Running for the elevators. Corey swerved wide around the old man. No time to confront him. He wouldn't be looking out for Corey anyway. He'd taken this time hop long before he knew Corey had the ability. As he entered the building, Corey lost sight of her.

No. There by the turnstiles. She was showing an ID card to a guard.

Corey sprinted after her, but a guard stepped in his way. He was smiling, calm, placid—*Why were they all so relaxed?* "Hello, son," he said. "Do you have a pass? Or an appointment?"

"That's my grandmother!" he said. "She . . . she forgot something!"

The guard looked over his shoulder and called out, "Ma'am?"

"Maria!" Corey called out, but she raced to the elevators without responding.

"Sorry, guy," the guard said, gesturing to a long desk against the wall. "Just come with me, give me your name, and pick up a pass. Sorry, but you can't be too careful these days!"

"Okay, listen to me," Corey said. "No one needs a pass right now. You need to get out of here—"

That was when he heard the boom above. The ground shook so hard he felt his teeth rattle and lost his footing. People fell to the floor around him. Screams rang out.

"What the heck?" the guard said, fishing out a walkie-talkie.

Corey leaped to his feet, ran to the turnstile, and jumped over it. Running toward the elevator, he called out his grandmother's name.

Above him, he heard a low, sickening crunch. The massive building shook like a subway train. He looked up in time to see a section of the ceiling explode into dust and tumble downward, directly over his head.

16

Leila hated not being able to remember her dreams. No matter how hard she tried, she couldn't do it. Ever. Not even one detail.

Most of the time, though, she could tell if they were good dreams or bad. Like that Saturday morning, when she woke up on the floor, screaming.

That was a really bad one.

"Leila, sweetie, did you have a nightmare?"

The first thing Leila saw when her eyes popped open was her mom's face covered in cucumber facial mud. "I'm having one now," she said. "My mother turned into a green raccoon."

Her mom puckered up her face and stuck out her tongue. A piece of cucumber mud flaked off and fell to the floor. "You scared me. You were really screaming."

Leila shrugged. "Sorry. I'm glad to be awake."

"Hungry for pancakes?"

"Sure. But if they taste like cucumber, I will barf."

With a weary laugh, her mom picked up the fallen piece and padded back toward the kitchen.

Leila sat on her bed. Her heart was galloping. She looked at her clock. 8:47. Her alarm was set to go off in thirteen minutes. Usually she loved sleeping late on Saturdays. But she knew she couldn't go back to sleep now.

Something was very wrong.

Her phone chimed, and she nearly leaped off the bed. Picking it up, she saw a push notification from her calendar: Rachel over for breakfast. 11:00 Drama Club.

"Mom?" she called out. "Can you make enough breakfast for Rachel, too? She's coming over!"

"I already knew that!" Mom replied.

Sitting back on her bed, Leila picked up her phone and texted Corey.

> hey. did it work?
> let me know when u get back!!!
> i'm worried.

After waiting a moment for a response that didn't come, she put her phone on her desk.

Leila tried to remember Papou's rules of time travel. Corey could leave today but arrive at a different date in another year. But no matter what day he traveled to, he'd always have to arrive at the same time of day.

She frowned, trying to burn those rules into her memory.

Date, year—could be different.

Time of day—has to be the same.

Which meant that wherever and whenever he landed, he'd be there around now, 8:47 a.m.

And if he made it to 9/11, he'd be there around the time the big disaster happened.

Leila could hear her mom mixing the pancake batter. She could smell bacon on the griddle. But she wasn't feeling hungry. She couldn't help pacing back and forth in her room, thinking about Corey. What if he died? Was it possible to die before you were even born? They never had quite figured that one out.

Or . . .

There was something else they hadn't figured out. Hadn't even talked about.

What if he did change the past? *How would she even know he did?* Wouldn't her memory instantly change to fit the new past? Like how she always remembered a Frederick Ruggles School—but Corey claimed there never was one, that *he* was the one who caused it to happen by changing the past.

It seemed that Throwbacks could remember the *before* and the *after*. But Leila only knew the *after*. It was like her memory just . . . adjusted.

Thoughts swirled in her head. Thoughts about Corey's grandmother. Leila knew she had died, and she knew Corey had gone into the past to save her. Okay, so what if he *saved* her, right now at 8:49 on that horrible day in 2001? What if he was racing up the West Side Highway with her, alive? Then if Corey changed the past, Leila's memory would change, too! She would remember that Corey's grandmother escaped the Twin Towers. She would be thinking that Corey's grandmother is alive and always has been!

But Leila wasn't feeling that at all. And that made her panic.

She looked at her phone. No answer from Corey.

She didn't want to assume anything. Time travel was not intuitive. It was impossible to make perfect sense of it. Maybe the memory adjustment took a while.

Maybe some memories were immune from adjustment.

Maybe if you *knew* about time travel, you no longer adjusted at all.

Maybe Corey was still in the process of his heroic rescue . . .

Maybe pigs flew . . .

Aaaaghh!

Leila hated going around in mental circles. There was only one way to find out if the old woman was alive. She called Corey's sister, Zenobia. The phone rang seven times. When Zenobia picked up, there was a long silence. "Hrrrjj . . ."

"Hey, Zenobe, it's Leila," she said. "Are you up? Quick question. Um. How's Corey?"

"No," Zenobia shot back. "That's the answer to your first question. Which was 'Are you up?' And the answer to your second is, Why don't you text him? I heard him leave this morning. I thought maybe he was eloping with you."

Leila felt her face turning red. "Anyway, this may seem weird," she said, ignoring the snarky comment, "but I'm doing . . . um, a genealogy project, and I wanted to ask a question about your grandmother."

"My grandmother?"

"Yes!" Leila's blood was pumping. "Like, when was

the last time you talked to her?"

"Let's see . . . ," she said. "About a week ago?"

This was not the answer Leila had expected. And she nearly screamed with joy. "A w-w-week?"

"Yeah. Why?"

"*That's amazing, Zenobe! That is just so awesome!*" She had to sit down on the bed. Corey had done it. He'd succeeded! She thrust her fist in the air and tried not to scream.

"I guess it's awesome . . . ," Zenobia said. "If you don't count the fact that she no longer remembers anyone's name and lives in a nursing home in Queens."

Leila sank back into her pillows. "I—I'm sorry. I didn't know that."

"Corey never told you?"

"No. That must be hard on you guys. Especially Papou."

"Papou?" Zenobia said. "Whoa, sorry. I thought you were talking about my other grandmother. My mom's mom. The one who's alive."

"Alive?" Leila said.

"Leila, you know my *yiayia* died on nine-eleven, right?" Zenobia scolded. "I always assumed Corey told you that."

"Right," Leila said. "Right. I . . . forgot. . . ."

"Are you okay? You sound weird."

"I—I have to go, Zenobia. Sorry."

"Wait. That's all you wanted to ask me?"

"If you see Corey, tell him to . . . to call me."

"What about your genealogy proj—?"

As Leila pressed the off button, her alarm began to sound. It was 9:00. She shut it and rose off the bed. Her breaths came in ragged gasps. The scheme hadn't worked. Corey's grandmother had been gone before Corey left, and she was still gone.

Long gone.

And what about Corey?

She let out a strangled shout. If only she could jump into the past herself, find out where he was. Tears blurred her vision. She told herself not to lose hope. He knew exactly when the planes would come. He wouldn't stick around past the time.

Would he?

Zenobia's suggestion to text him made a weird kind of sense. Texts to Corey might be useful. She could remind him about what had happened today, in Central Park. About his brave trip into the past. For now the text would just hang in cyberspace. But if—when— Corey returned, they'd appear on his phone.

And if, by some miracle, he did rescue his grand-mother, then Leila's memory would be adjusted. She wouldn't even know Corey went into the past. But her texts would be there, and Corey could read them to her. And then she'd know. There would be a record of *before. She was dead and then she was alive. Because of Corey.*

She picked up her phone and looked at her messages. Still nothing back from Corey. So she began to type:

corey, I'm still worried. just wanted to say,
as of 9am u r back in the past &
have not returned.
yr grandmother died on 911 but u went
2 try 2 save her. so far that is still a fact.
I hope when u return she will b alive.
and if my memory of that is gone I hope
this text will stay on yr phone so I can
know what a hero u r. but most of all
I want to see u again. dont b dead lol.
pls write as soon as u can.
Xoxoxox

She sent it, then thought twice and wrote another one.

> no matter what happens,
> u r still a hero in my book anyway

As she sent that one, she smelled something burning. "Mom?" she called out. "Is everything okay in there?"

"Just murdered a few slices of bacon, sorry!" her mother called back. "I'm useless without you. Want to help me whip some cream?"

Leila pocketed her phone. As she headed for the door, her foot clipped one of Auntie Flora's boxes. It toppled over, sending the contents sprawling. The lacquer box with the skating scene, still locked tight, landed upside down.

Leila quickly picked it up. It was warm in her hand, even though the morning was chilly. As she gazed at the skating scene, it seemed to grow even warmer.

She nearly dropped it.

Placing the box carefully on her desk, she called out, "Mom, can you give me a couple of minutes?"

17

As Corey awakened, there was only one thought in his mind:

She's dead.

He spat out dust. His arm ached, his pants were ripped, and a rat was nibbling on his shoelace.

"Yecchh!" he cried, pulling in his leg.

The critter gave him a steady, disappointed look and then scampered into a hole in the dirt. Corey coughed and blinked the dust from his eyes. He tried to sit up but he was knocked back by the pain all over his body. He blinked and looked upward. Two vertical dirt walls arose on either side of him, maybe twenty feet high, framing a clear sky. The soil below him was wet and smelled foul.

He had no idea what had just happened or where he was. Had he fallen into some ditch that was safe from the World Trade Center debris? Had someone pulled him to a construction site across the highway?

No matter what, he was alone. Which meant he'd been too late. She'd run past him. Up to her office. She'd been in the elevator when it happened. Corey felt like a murderer. What good was being a Throwback if you couldn't take advantage of the powers? It was an epic fail. A fatal fail. He was alive—somewhere—and she wasn't.

He heard a low moan, slowly rising to a shout. It took a few seconds to realize that it had come from his own mouth.

"Sounds like a bloody animal," came a voice from above him. "Madam, is this the young ruffian who attacked you?"

Corey scrambled to his feet. From above the wall, an old man stared down at him through a monocle. He had thick white sideburns and wore a brimmed hat. "What the— Who are you?" Corey blurted out.

"The fascination is mutual, I assure you," the man said.

He was joined by a woman with thick makeup and dyed red hair that peeked out of the edges of a kerchief. "The kid didn't attack, he jes' appeeahed outta nowheah," she replied, in the thickest New York accent Corey had ever heard. "Fell in, boom. He wuzn't fresh or nothin'. Say, are yuz okay, young fella?"

Corey didn't know how to reply. He blinked and looked around in bewilderment. Not far from him were two men lying against the dirt wall in the shadows, surrounded by empty bottles. They stared at him with bleary, half-lidded eyes.

"I think the lady likes ya, Stretch," one of them called out to Corey in a thick and slurry voice.

"Send 'er to me if she wants a real man," growled the other guy.

"Send 'er to you if she wants to lose whatever money she has."

"Ahhhh, yer mudder's mustache."

"Ahhhh, yer fadder's belly button."

Neither of the men moved a muscle while speaking. Now it looked like they were falling asleep, as if that little conversation was enough work for the day. There were other men behind them. No one seemed to be doing much of anything. Some were standing, some lying down.

The gash of daylight overhead showed a calm, clear sky. No debris, no fires, no dust clouds, no eerie silence.

None of the things people described about the 9/11 aftermath. The wall behind Corey was perfectly vertical, supported in places by thick wood planks. It was separated from the parallel wall by about sixty yards of flat, hard-packed dirt floor. Which meant Corey was in a ditch—a roofless tunnel that stretched as far as he could see, lined here and there with rickety ladders.

But . . . *where was this?*

Corey was seized with panic. The sharp pop of a nearby explosion made him flinch. One of the ditch people let out a hoot, shouting, "Here comes Tin Lizzie! Give her a proper greetin'!"

A group of men lumbered over to a bridge that spanned the ditch overhead, a thick set of wood planks supported by a rickety metal scaffold. Across it, a clunky old black car puttered loudly, making the planks bow dangerously downward. The men jeered and made fart noises, waving their hats and laughing. From inside the car, a proper-looking woman with a powdered-white face stared wide-eyed for a moment and then rolled up her window.

"I say, boy!" called the old man directly above Corey. "Can I get someone to give you a hand and deliver you from these thieving rapscallions?"

"What?" Corey said. "Sure."

As the man and woman disappeared, Corey slumped against the wall. What had just happened? He was not in 2001, that was clear. But where was he—and *when*?

Corey spotted his grandmother's schedule and his ancestor's passport at his feet, and he stooped to pick them up. The passport was open to the photo. Corey smiled down at the stern old face. The man whose name day brought Maria Harvoulakis Fletcher to the Greek church and *almost* saved her life. "Worst happy name day ever, huh?" he said grimly, unfolding the cover to close it.

A moment later, the old man and the red-haired woman reappeared above him. With them was a guy in a cap, overalls, and a striped shirt who looked like a younger version of Popeye. He tipped his cap at Corey, lay flat on his torso, and reached a hand down. "Alley-oop, pal! Grab one of them ladders that ain't broken."

Corey did as he was told, and a moment later he was scrabbling over the edge of the ditch. "Atta boy," the guy said. "Name's Rusty."

"I'm Mildred but everybody calls me Millie," the woman said. She curtsied awkwardly, her dress flouncing left and right.

"I'm Filcher," the old man said.

Corey looked around in bafflement. He was

surrounded by four-story brick buildings, but it looked like someone had bulldozed a wide path right through them to make the ditch. Piles of construction rubble were everywhere, and some of the buildings were even missing corners, like they'd been sliced. Apartment interiors showed through the broken walls, their flowered wallpaper making them look like giant abandoned dollhouses. "I'm Corey."

"What the heck were you doin' down there with them rummies, kid?" Rusty said.

"He fell in, Einstein, whaddya think?" said Millie. "A lotta people fall in."

The old man shook his head. He reached into his coat pocket, pulled out a white card, and handed it to Corey. "Outrageous! This foolish subway construction is the height of negligence. They evict good citizens from their homes, destroy the buildings, take their merry time building their track, and then—surprise! The war effort requires steel, so construction is halted. And what's left? A public hole! A breeding ground for vermin and immorality! A death trap after dark! And for what—to lay down tracks and extend the subway into Brooklyn? Who on earth wants to go to Brooklyn in a tube under the river? Who will ever need that?"

"Me, for one," Rusty said. "I live there."

As the two men bickered, Corey peered behind the big man, at a sign that had been pasted to a brick wall:

!!ATTENTION!!
NEIGHBORS! FRIENDS!!!

WHEREAS, the corrupt City Government has decided without Consult to extend the Seventh Avenue Subway below 14th Street and into the City of Brooklyn, and

WHEREAS, the need for Steel to provide Ammunition for our heroic Troops in the Great War has halted Construction, and

WHEREAS, the dastardly Gash that mars our Village has been allowed to remain open like a Festering Wound due to the Bribes and Extortion paid to the Fat Cats of Tammany, and

WHEREAS, the good People of Greenwich Village have lost their Lives due to Falls & the attendant Cracked Skulls, **THEN**

LET IT BE RESOLVED that we the Suffering shall **RISE UP** to rectify this Injustice!!! Join us!!!

UNION SQUARE
6:00 P.M.
JUNE 15, 1917

"Wait," Corey said. "Are you serious? It's 1917? How the heck did that happen?"

His head was throbbing. This made no sense.

"Whot, whot?" the old man said. "Disorientation, memory loss—these indicate brain injury! Once again, industrial progress claims an innocent victim! But you, young fellow, are in luck, for I am an attorney! I represent the concerns of the good citizens of Greater Greenwich Village, who have suffered from this god-forsaken construction project. And I am, humbly, at your service."

Corey read the man's card:

HORACE P. FILCHER, ESQUIRE

ATTORNEY AT LARGE
345 ½ HUDSON STREET
NEW YORK 4, NEW YORK
THOUGHTFUL · THOROUGH · THRIFTY

"Thanks," Corey said.

"Young man, I instruct you to clean yourself up," Filcher replied. "I will expect to see you in my offices as soon as you can. It will be to our mutual financial benefit, I assure you. And whom shall I expect? The full name is Corey . . ."

"Fletcher," Corey replied.

The man extended a bony hand. "Fletcher, I'm Filcher. *Haa!* That's a good omen. Visit anytime from nine to five. Except from twelve thirty to two thirty, when I have my postprandial detour into the arms of Morpheus."

"Sounds illegal," Rusty said.

"It means he's napping," Millie piped up. "Such a fancy pants."

Tipping his hat, the old man walked away. "Good day, all."

"Aaayy, just a second!" Rusty followed right after him, his face growing red. "Where's the quarter you said you'd pay me for helpin' out?"

"I must, erm, collect some debts first. . . ."

As Corey watched them go, Millie put her arm around him. "You gonna be okay, big guy? You got a place to go?"

Corey nodded. "I'm fine," he lied.

"Well, I'll be at the market on Christopher if ya need me."

Blowing a kiss to Corey, she walked uptown. Corey was relieved to be alone. He glanced up and down the street. It wasn't much of one, really, just the big ditch surrounded by debris. On either side were the remnants of destroyed buildings. Side streets, lined with gas lamps, retreated from sight. Where those side streets intersected the hole, rickety bridges had been built. People were trying to walk carefully across, ignoring the catcalls and noises from the gang below. The women were in long dresses, the men in loose-fitting shabby pants and shirts. Nearly everyone wore hats of some kind, and all the clothes seemed to be some shade of brown, gray, or black. Makeshift street signs had been put up at each block. Corey was at Morton Street and could see that the next block was Barrow—streets that still existed in the twenty-first century. They were nowhere near the World Trade Center site. Just as Filcher had said, it was the West Village.

The crack of a whip made him spin around. A horse was trotting toward him, pulling a wagon piled with garbage. "Outta my way, boy!" the driver shouted, his mouth missing so many teeth that it looked like a piano keyboard.

Corey had to get somewhere quieter, less dangerous, less bombed-out. He ran up the avenue, over piles of rubble, and turned up Barrow Street. It was paved with cobblestones and lined with neat brick and stone buildings. But garbage was strewn in the gutter, and the air reeked of horse poop. He stopped in mid-block, at an empty lot. An older couple was sitting on the stoop of the brownstone next door, and they stopped their conversation to give him a curious look.

His breaths were shallow, panicked. The shock was wearing off, and questions flooded into his brain. Why was he *here*? Why wasn't he back in the present? You needed metal. Steel, nickel, copper, gold, silver. He didn't have any 1917 coins or subway tokens or belt buckles. Just coins from the present and . . .

A passport.

Could that be it?

Believe it or not, often a photograph alone will do, because of the silver content, Papou had said.

Quickly Corey reached into his pocket for the passport of his great-great-grandfather-of-the-unpronounceable name, Evanthis Harvoulakis. Once again he opened it.

The date under the photo was June 9, 1917. Corey had been holding on to it when the first plane hit the World Trade Center. He looked closely at the face. It was clearer, less yellow than it had been in 2001. Brandnew and warm to the touch.

Corey was alive. Because of Evanthis.

He hadn't saved his grandmother. But *her* grandfather had saved him.

"Thanks, E.," Corey whispered. Talking to the image of his ancestor made him feel weirdly sane. "Hey, I know you're around here, somewhere, at the same time as me. That's cool. In case I don't get the chance to meet you, which I probably won't, I just want to say I'm sorry. I let you down. I didn't save your granddaughter. I mean, I know that doesn't make sense. In 1917 you don't have a granddaughter yet. And you probably died before 2001, so you have no idea what I'm talking about—I mean, you *wouldn't* have an idea if you could hear me. Which you can't. Because you're a photograph . . ."

Now the old couple were staring at him, slack-jawed. Corey smiled tightly. "Gotta go! Have a nice day!"

He ducked into the empty lot and pressed himself to the side wall of the brownstone, hidden from sight. He had to get back home and talk to Papou. He wanted to try 2001 again. With better planning.

Hopping to 1917 was an accident, but getting home shouldn't be too hard. He was a veteran time-hopper now, with four hops under his belt—on his block, in Central Park, at the World Trade site, here. Papou said it got easier and easier to do. Corey was glad he'd brought coins and his cell phone, all the metal he'd ever need.

He reached into his pocket. His fingers closed around a Snickers wrapper and a pack of tissues.

He checked the other pocket. Empty.

What?

He tried again. He scoured the sidewalk in case they'd spilled out. He'd been dropping a lot of stuff lately. But he saw no coins. No money at all. No phone. Not even the 2001 subway token.

His stomach seized up. He ran back out to Barrow Street. He followed his path to the ditch. As he got to the edge, he looked over. The two drunken men were awake now, trying to build a fire using newspapers. One of them glanced up. "Uh-oh . . ."

"We didn't do nothin'," the other protested. "It was Hans."

"And Benny-boy," the first guy said. "They both got sticky fingers. Said you was carryin' a lot of scratch. And other interesting stuff."

"They—they pickpocketed me?" Corey cried out. "When I was unconscious?"

The first guy shook his head in sympathy. "A sleeping kid. Imagine that! No morals. We'd never do that. We got mannerisms."

"Do you know where they went?" Corey asked.

"The ones who took my money?"

The two men shared a look. Then they piped up at the same time, as if it were the most obvious thing in the world:

"To spend it!"

18

Corey checked the address on the old lawyer's business card against the number on the tiny brick building—345½ Hudson Street.

The door was tilted, the building narrow. Its rows of brick, instead of going straight across the front, sagged downward toward the middle. It was as if the two apartment buildings on either side had expanded toward each other, squeezing the little house between them. Just above the door, on a rusted metal hook, dangled a wooden shingle that said H. P. FILCHER, ESQ., ATTORNEY AT L.

It looked like termites had gotten to the *AW*.

Corey knocked on the door once . . . twice. Finally he heard the heavy thumping of footsteps on the other side. But the door did not open. Instead a weirdly high-pitched voice called from within: "Helloooo! This is Mr. Filcher's secretary! Consultation by appointment only!"

"Uh, this is Corey Fletcher?" Corey said.

"Is that a question?" the voice said tentatively. "How would I know who you are?"

"No, it's a statement!" Corey said.

"I heard a question mark at the end. It sounded to me definitely like a—"

"I'm identifying myself!" Corey interrupted. "I met Mr. Filcher a little earlier today? I'm the victim of a theft. I don't have an appointment but he said I could see him anytime from—"

The door swung open. Instead of some dotty old woman, it was Filcher himself. The bags under his eyes had deepened. He was no longer wearing a hat, and his hair was all bunched up on one side, brittle and white. "Ah, yes, I know exactly who you are!" he said.

"Wait, that voice . . . it was you?" Corey said.

"Yes, well, you see, my . . . uh, staff is out ill today, so to fend off all the inquiries . . . you know how it is . . . popularity," Filcher said. "Come. Sit. Are you injured? Headaches? Double vision? Triple vision? The courts are very sympathetic to triple vision."

He led Corey down a dark, narrow corridor. A string of bare light bulbs hung overhead, but only one of them was working. At the end of the hall, they stepped into an office. Corey couldn't tell if it was small or large. There wasn't much to see besides piles and piles of papers jammed together, rising practically to the ceiling like a city skyline. A pathway snaked through them, leading to a desk and a metal file cabinet, both of which seemed to have papers growing out of them. Perched atop the unruly pile on the cabinet, a metal fan whined noisily but generated no breeze.

Filcher pushed a fat, bored-looking black cat off one of the massive stacks. As he lifted the papers off and shifted them to his desk, he revealed a hidden chair that looked like it hadn't seen a human butt in years. "Sit. Sit! Make yourself at home!" Filcher said. "Ignore the untidiness. My cleaning staff is—"

"Out ill," Corey said. "I know. Thanks for seeing me, sir."

Filcher sat in a worn leather seat behind his desk and leaned toward Corey. "Unlike most attorneys, my boy, I let my clients call me by my first name. You see, I have three names—Mr. Horace Filcher. So you can call me . . . Mr. Filcher. Haaa! You see what I did there?"

172

Corey stared at him, speechless.

"Yes, well, this is what we call breaking the ice," Filcher said. "Loosening up. Always room for humor, eh? Go on."

"Okay, so you were right about those guys in the ditch," Corey said. "You called them thieving. And that's what they did. They stole all my money while I was unconscious. All my possessions!"

"I see . . . ," Filcher said, stroking his sideburns thoughtfully. "You know, judges are very generous with a combination of memory loss and double vision—"

"This is about theft!" Corey said.

"No, this is about compensation!" Filcher pounded his desk, sending up a cloud of dust. "I happen to be one of New York County's most reputable personal injury attorneys. If you follow my line of thinking, my lad, you will be sure to get more money than you lost! Er, how much did you lose?"

Corey had to cough out a lungful of dust before he could reply. There was no way he could explain why he needed the coins, or what a cell phone was. "Well . . . the amount isn't the important thing."

"True," Filcher said, "we can round up generously."

"Is there any way we could get back exactly what

I lost, sir—I mean, not an equal amount but the exact coins?"

Filcher sat back, his brow furrowed. "That's an unusual request. But brilliant in its own way. We may be able to do this quickly, without involving the courts at all." The lawyer leaped from his seat, grabbing his jacket. "These thieves tend to go to one place. Follow me."

Haak's Pawnshop was marked by a faded sign above cement stairs that led down to a dark basement entrance. As Corey descended behind Filcher, he nearly gagged at the stink. "That's disgusting," he said, pinching his nostrils. "Doesn't he have a bathroom inside?"

"You get used to it," Filcher said. "The smell is kind of a filter, you see. Only serious customers will endure it, and Haak likes his buyers motivated."

The door at the bottom was thick with layers of paint and festooned with signs: BEWARE DOG!! MARKSMAN INSIDE!! SHOPLIFTERS SHOT ON SIGHT!! PUBLIC URINATORS SHOT TWICE!!!

"Don't be dissuaded," Filcher said, pushing the door open. "Haak is a puppy dog. And none of these warnings are true."

"I figured that out," Corey said.

As they entered, Corey slammed the door hard behind him.

"HORACE, YOU OLD HORSE-TRADING, BOOT-LICKING, LYING SKINFLINT, HOW DO YOU INTEND TO CHEAT ME TODAY?"

A thickly accented voice bellowed from inside, so violently loud that Corey almost had the urge to open the door and leave. Instead he turned to see a man with a girth so wide he could have swallowed a small bus. He waddled out from behind a long glass display case, wearing a white tank-top T-shirt soaked with sweat. A pair of threadbare suspenders stretched over his torso so tightly you could almost hear them groan. His face was perfectly round, his cheeks red and juicy like beef patties not yet cooked. On his shiny head was a single tuft of blond hair shaped like a question mark. Despite the harsh words, he was smiling broadly at Filcher.

"Good morning, Haak," Filcher said quietly, shrinking away. "But please spare my tender, crooked back. Whatever you do, please do not strike—"

With an open palm the size of a dinner plate, the man smacked Filcher on his back and sent him staggering to the wall. "Love this guy!" he said, turning to Corey with his hand extended. "Otto Haak! Welcome!

Don't tell me Horace the Miser hired an assistant!"

Corey backed away, tucking his hands behind his back. "Corey Fletcher. I'm not his assistant."

"The boy . . . is a . . . client . . . ," Filcher said through gritted teeth, holding his back with his right hand. "Has been . . . robbed."

Corey's eyes swept around the shop. It was larger and neater than he expected, its walls lined with floor-to-ceiling glass cases displaying typewriters, vases, bowls, silverware, plates, binoculars, eyeglasses, odd contraptions Corey didn't recognize, and jewelry. Lots of jewelry.

There was one other customer, a handsome, apple-cheeked guy in his teens or twenties. He was wearing a tan, wide-brimmed cowboy hat, a bright plaid shirt with a string tie, a leather vest, loose jeans, and cowboy boots. At his feet were a beat-up old canvas satchel and a coiled rope. He tipped his hat to Corey, revealing thick, slicked-down brown hair. "Robbed, huh?" he said. "Hoo-ee, sorry to hear that, Corey Filcher. Back home, they told me if you didn't want to lose your money in New York City, you had to sew it to your skin! Guess they was right!"

Corey smiled for the first time that day. "I'm Fletcher, he's Filcher."

The guy burst out laughing. "Now that's funny. This whole city's like a burlesque show, ain't it? I'm Quinn. Quinn Roper. From Casper, Wyoming."

"Haak, my good man," Filcher said, ignoring the conversation, "the theft in question befell my client a mere hour or so ago. After an unfortunate fall into the pit of doom that has split our fair neighborhood—"

"The cursed Seventh Avenue subway!" Haak spat. "We need that like we need a hole into the head."

"It's in," Quinn Roper said. "Hole in the head."

"So there he was, an unconscious and helpless boy of eleven," Filcher said, rising to his full height and gripping his lapel, "discovered by the lazy, drunken, immoral dregs of our fair city—in other words, your customers, Haak. And they, rather than show the decency we are used to in the higher classes, brutally set upon him and tore the possessions from his very pockets. Every last cent."

Haak's eyes had grown moist. "You always had a way with words, you old grifter."

"Mr. Filcher, I'm not eleven," Corey whispered. "I'm—"

Filcher elbowed Corey in the ribs. "I put myself at your mercy, Haak," he barreled on, "on behalf of this innocent, orphaned babe with not a cent to his name."

"Orphaned? Oh . . ." Now Haak was openly sobbing.

Quinn gave Corey a silent, quizzical look, and Corey shook his head. *Not true.*

"Don't let anyone say Haak ain't got a heart," Haak said. "You can sleep on the floor, kid. Nice and warm. And I can give you work. I need a boy to take out the chamber pot, kill the vermin, clean up the spit—"

"He doesn't need that!" Filcher leaned over the counter. "He needs money. As do I. I send you customers, Haak. They bring priceless goods—"

"*Stolen* goods," Haak pointed out.

"Which you cheerfully sell. And from which you owe me a cut. I calculate your debts to me have risen to seven hundred ninety-three dollars and thirteen cents!"

"I can't pay that!"

"I'll take half," Filcher replied, "or expect the full weight of the New York court system on your shady enterprise. Now, tell me, Corey, the name of the thieves were . . ."

"Hans and Benny-boy," Corey offered.

"Regulars," Haak grumbled. He lumbered around behind a glass-topped desk, pulled a fistful of dollars out of a drawer, and spread them out on the case. "A bunch of those fellas did come in to buy. Told me they inherited some cash from a wealthy aunt. Of course I didn't believe them. But greenbacks is greenbacks. Go ahead. This is all I can give you, Filcher!"

Corey eyed the bills, but he wasn't really interested in them. "What about coins? Did they bring any coins?"

"Of course they did," Haak said, pulling open a drawer behind the desk.

Corey peered over. The drawer was deep and wide. It was piled at least two feet high with pennies, nickels, dimes, and quarters. Thousands of them. There was no way in the world he would find a random coin from the twenty-first century.

Haak dug his fleshy hand into the pile, pulled out a fistful of coins, and dumped them on the table next to the bills. "There!" Haak said.

"How about a weird subway token?" Corey said. "Did they return anything like that?"

"A what?" Haak replied.

"Or—or a little metal gizmo? With a digital clock and a selfie on it?"

Haak shook his head, staring at Corey as if he'd just spoken in Sanskrit. Quinn was staring at him, too.

Filcher quickly leaned across the counter, sliding all the bills and coins toward him. "Thank you, Haak, you are the soul of compassion and gullibility."

"It's my sweet, generous nature," Haak said with a modest smile, as Filcher dumped all the money into a valise.

Quinn glared at the old man. "Hey, what about Fletcher?"

"I don't know how they do it in Montana, young man," Filcher sniffed, "but here in civilized society the attorney collects the money, extracts his proper fee, then pays the client his share."

"Wyoming!" Quinn protested.

"Same thing." Filcher turned to the door, hooking the valise over his shoulder. "Come now, Fletcher, before I choke on the smell of stupidity."

19

Leila examined the lacquer box, holding it in two hands. The warmth of the wood was a great contrast to the cheerful, wintry skating scene painted on the top. It was so vivid and lifelike, Leila could practically hear the ringing of bells.

Actually, she *was* hearing the ringing of bells. Someone was at the door.

She set the box on her desk. The warmth of the wood made her curious about what Auntie Flora kept in there, but the thick brass hasp held tight. In its center was a small round keypad with buttons labeled 1 through 6.

She would have to investigate later.

"Leila, Rachel's here!" her mother called.

Leila turned toward the door, checking her phone once more for a message from Corey. None. She thought about his grandmother. In Leila's memory, she was still dead. That had not changed.

But maybe it would. There was still a chance that Corey would pull off a rescue. Leila wished she knew more history, like exactly how long it took for the buildings to collapse and how soon the survivors started to run away.

She ran out toward the front door, just as it swung open and Rachel bounded in.

"What's up?" Leila asked.

Rachel staggered past her and clomped into Leila's bedroom, flopping on the bed. "I am so trashed from that party!"

"The Diet Cokes were killer," Leila said, following her in.

"I mean the dancing!" As Rachel kicked off her shoes, she spotted Leila's new discovery. "Nice lacquer box!"

"It's my aunt's."

"My dad brought one home from Moscow once," Rachel said. "Anything inside it?"

Leila shrugged. "I don't know. I can't open it."

Rachel fiddled with the lock, pressing random

numbers. She glanced up with a mischievous smile. "Do we *want* to know?"

"Yeah. I guess."

"We can crack this. It's only six numbers. That means only six factorial choices, which would be . . ." Rachel thought a moment. "Seven hundred twenty possible combinations, assuming the combo itself has six numbers."

"I hate math geeks," Leila said.

"I know, especially if they're hot. And funny." Rachel sighed. "I guess I would hate me, too."

Leila threw a pillow at her. Rachel fell back on the bed, giggling and kicking her feet in the air. Leila noticed a crisscrossing of scratches on her left ankle. "What happened to you?"

Rachel grimaced. "Catsquatch attacked. Can you believe it? I think it was offended by your Catwoman costume. I had to explain I wasn't you. You know, to cats, all humans look alike."

"Ha ha," Leila said.

A waft of buttery blueberry pancake smell sighed into the room, and Rachel jumped off the bed. "*Gee, Leila,*" she said in a loud voice, "*we better go help your mom make breakfast!*"

"Nice try for points, kid, but they're done!" Leila's

mom called back. "Come and get 'em!"

Rachel winked at Leila and ran out of the room. Leila checked the phone one more time. Nothing from Corey.

Taking a deep breath, she put it in her pocket and followed her friend.

Catsquatch, aka Jabba the Cat, was waiting outside when the two girls left. As the door opened it sprang to its feet and bared its teeth.

Rachel screamed, unhooking her backpack and waving it at the little beast. "Back! Back! Away, violent beast!"

"Rrrrrrr," said Catsquatch.

"Maybe if you were nice to it, it wouldn't attack you." Leila smiled at the white cat. "Awww, don't pay attention to Rachel. She loves kitty cats."

"This isn't a kitty," Rachel murmured. "It's a monster."

Catsquatch shot Rachel a glance, bared its teeth, and looked longingly at Leila.

"Did you see that?" Rachel cried out. "It understood me!"

Leila had to admit that did freak her out. But animals could be very intuitive. "Let's just go."

They went left and walked up Central Park West. Rachel began reciting her lines to the play they were rehearsing, *Into the Woods*. It wasn't until they'd crossed Ninety-Seventh Street that Leila felt something touch the back of her left shoe.

She spun around.

Inches behind her, Catsquatch sat back on its haunches.

"This. Can't. Be. Happening," Rachel muttered.

But the white cat was ignoring her, staring straight up at Leila. It raised its right paw. "I think it wants a handshake," Leila said.

"Go for it if you want," Rachel said. "Be BFFs! Start dating. But don't be late for rehearsal. I'm out of here."

As she turned to go, the cat slapped its paw firmly down on the sidewalk.

Then it repeated the same motion. And again. And again.

The whole time its eyes never left Leila's. There was something human about them, almost familiar. "Are you trying to tell me something?" Leila whispered.

Catsquatch's head went up and down, like a nod. It hissed, and Leila could swear it was saying *yessssss*.

Just as before, it lifted its paw and slapped it down— only this time, thrice.

"Four . . ." Leila said. "And three . . . ? What are you telling me?"

"*Leila—come on!*" Rachel shouted from up the block.

Now Catsquatch tapped five times.

And two.

"Four. Three. Five. Two," Leila said.

"*What are you doing?*"

"I think it's communicating with us!"

"*Auuugggggh! See you there, and don't blame me if they fire you!*"

But Leila's eyes were fixed on the cat. "So, four, three, five, two? That's what you're trying to tell me? And you want me to figure out what that means? Like, maybe a combination to something?"

Catsquatch held its head high. Although Leila knew it wasn't possible, it looked like the cat was smiling.

20

Corey wished he'd had more experience with law-yers, because it didn't feel like 10 percent was a fair share of the money from Haak. But that was all Filcher would give him.

Not that it made any difference. None of the coins was from the twenty-first century anyway. In Filcher's office, Corey had at least been able to check the dates on them. Which meant he was stuck.

"Cheer up, it's better than nothing!" Quinn said brightly, as the two walked down Greenwich Street. "Thirteen dollars and seventy-two cents? Heck, I wouldn't sneeze at that."

"You wouldn't?" Corey said glumly. He felt the coins jingling in his pocket. How long before the money would run out? Then what—just live out life in 1917? Never see his parents or Zenobia or Leila or Papou again?

"No, sir, my dad makes less than that in a month!" Quinn declared. He was trying to make conversation, trying to be cheerful. But all Corey wanted to do was scream. Or jump in the river. "Anyways, me and the old man? We don't get along too good no more. One day at the train depot I see this sign: 'Cowboys needed, New York City, good pay.' I figure it's a mistake because it's so strange, but I check the words and it ain't. Well, heck, I say to myself, why not? Always wanted to visit the big city. So I sneak out. I got no money, but I make my way across the country hitching rides. To survive, I do *everything*—rodeos, magic tricks, ventriloquism, hypnotism, evangelism, all the isms you can think of. And here I am! Dirt poor but bright-eyed and bushy-tailed. Yee-HAH, I love the energy of this city! How about you?"

"I—I can't do this . . . ," Corey muttered. "You have too much energy. And I have never in my life heard a real person say yee-hah and mean it."

Quinn gave him a curious look. Then he pulled a penny out of his pocket and flipped it high into the air. "You need some food in your belly. Lunch is on the loser. Heads or tails?"

"Heads," Corey said.

Quinn caught the penny as it came down. It was heads. "Aw, shoot, I lose." He looked ahead to the end of the block, where an old guy was selling fruits and vegetables from a cart near the corner of Spring Street. Workers were emerging from a couple of nearby factory buildings, and a line had already formed in front of the cart. Quinn smiled. "Hee-hee. Watch this."

In a few lightning-quick movements, he unhooked the satchel from his shoulder and pulled out a long rope and a floppy little dalmatian dog doll. "Say howdy to Rex."

"Howdy to Rex," Corey murmured.

Quinn hooked the satchel back over his shoulder, tied the rope around Rex's neck, and dropped him to the sidewalk. Grabbing the other end of the rope, he walked toward Spring Street, whistling.

The rope was long. Quinn was almost to the fruit cart when the little doll started bouncing along after him. And barking.

Corey jumped back. The sound was high-pitched, sharp, and loud.

Quinn spun around. "Shush, Rex!"

For the first time all day, Corey laughed. This kid had been serious about being a ventriloquist. He really did know how to throw his voice.

The moment Quinn passed by the cart, the barking started again. Behind his back, Quinn was jerking the rope so that it looked like Rex was jumping up and down. Doing somersaults. Howling.

One by one, the people in line stared at the dog and began laughing—until even the dour old fruit peddler was doubled over. Corey couldn't believe it. The trick was really kind of corny. Yet everyone seemed to think it was the funniest thing on earth.

Finally, to a smattering of applause, Quinn scooped up Rex and scooted away from the cart. "Hurry!" he whispered to Corey, breaking into a run.

That was when an apple fell out of Quinn's satchel and rolled down the sidewalk.

"Hey! You!" the vendor shouted. "Thief! *Thief! Stop him!*"

Corey took off after Quinn. Now he saw that the satchel was bulging. Quinn's act had been a distraction. He could do ventriloquism *and* sleight of hand!

As the two boys sprinted toward Vandam Street, Corey couldn't help laughing. *"Dude, you didn't need to do that!"* he called out.

"Yee-HAH! It was fun!" Quinn replied, racing around the corner and out of sight.

Corey followed close behind, but he had to stop in his tracks. Quinn had face-planted in the dark-blue uniform of a very sturdy policeman.

The man was at least six feet four. He smiled through a brush-handle mustache, tapping a wooden club in his hand. Two other cops sat on horses in the street nearby. All of them were just outside a stable with a sign that read NEW YORK CITY POLICE.

"Bad choice . . ." Quinn murmured.

"Glad you had yer fun, laddies," the cop replied. "I'm Officer Blunt, and this is where fun goes to die."

The old fruit vendor muttered bitterly as he pulled apples, pears, bananas, and carrots out of Quinn's pack. Corey sat with his back to the wall, near the cart. He and Quinn hadn't moved an inch from where the police had told them to stay.

"Sorry," Quinn said. "My fault. I get a little crazy sometimes. They're not going to put us in jail, are they?"

"They don't put kids in jail for stealing fruit," Corey said. "At least they don't in the twenty-first—" He managed to close his mouth before the word *century* escaped. "Precinct!"

Officer Blunt was chatting with the vendor. He was also examining the fruit, eating some and occasionally tossing some to the two other officers for their horses. "They ain't paying," Quinn said. "How come they can do it and we can't?"

"There will be laws against that someday," Corey said.

"Oh, will there be?" Officer Blunt called out, sauntering over with his mouth full of apple. "You're a fortune-teller, eh? And from what Luigi the fruit guy tells me, your buddy is a comedian and a thief. Maybe he can tell a nice joke while you predict the color of your jail cell walls. I'll give you a hint. We don't use paint. *Hahhh!*"

The other officers all burst out laughing.

Blunt squatted next to Corey and Quinn. Flecks of half-eaten apple flew from his mouth as he spoke. "I'm just joshin' you boys," he said. "How old are youse?"

Quinn straightened his back against the wall. "Eighteen. Both of us."

"Heh, ya can't fool me, sonny," Blunt said. "Yer voice ain't changed yet. Still high, like a boy's. Tell me, you two have homes? Jobs? Any kind of identification? 'Cause I'm inclined to go lenient on youse if I know youse ain't street kids. These days, with the gangs running out of the Seventh Avenue subway Gash . . ."

"I live uptown with my family," Corey said, which

wasn't exactly a lie. He pulled the passport from his pocket. "This is my . . . father."

Blunt smiled and shook his head. "Greek fellas. They all look alike, don't they? And you, cowboy?"

"I just got here," Quinn said, pulling a folded sheet of paper from his pocket. "Tomorrow I'm going to try to get one of these jobs."

Blunt unfolded the sheet. As he held it at arm's length, Corey read it, too:

WANTED

WEST SIDE COWBOYS
NEW YORK CITY, NEW YORK

Young Men, ages **EIGHTEEN TO TWENTY-FIVE**, are Encouraged to apply for dangerous but VERY WELL-PAYING JOB. Expert Horse-Handling Skills required, as well as Familiarity with Lasso and Whip. Must be comfortable riding in front of moving Train, and clearing Track of Any Impediment! Room, Board, and ample Compensation!

CONTACT
R. LYME, PIER 66, NEW YORK 16, NEW YORK

"Mmm," Blunt said with a slight nod. "Well, I hope you're serious. The city needs all the hands we can get. Trains is running up the West Side, hauling cargo, day and night—but nobody's making deliveries on time, on account of all the drunks here and also up in the Tenderloin. They spill out of the bars, singing and happy, and they pass out on the tracks. Sometimes the drivers sees 'em but other times it's *toot-tooooot* . . . *splat!* If you catch my drift."

"I think I'm going to hurl," Corey said.

"My horse skills are second to none," Quinn said. "I know horses better 'n I know people. I ride 'em and raise 'em. Only thing I don't do is teach 'em how to speak."

"Impressive." Blunt smiled. "So I'm assuming you . . . eighteen-year-olds are not in school and need a job. Is this correct?"

Corey looked uncertainly at Quinn. "Yes, sir."

"Well, until you find employment on the tracks," Blunt said, "we could use you at the precinct house—mucking out stalls, grooming, exercising the horses, riding them from precinct to precinct as needed."

Quinn sprang to his feet. "We accept!"

"We?" Corey murmured.

"Excellent!" Officer Blunt said, then gestured toward

the fruit guy. "Luigi, some lunch for the two young gentlemen, courtesy of New York's Finest!"

"Yee-HAH!" Quinn cried out, leaping to his feet.

"Uh, just FYI," Corey murmured as he stood up, "I don't know how to ride."

Quinn looked at him as if he'd just admitted to being a potted plant. The two boys eyed the cops, who were now gathered at the cart, just out of earshot. "Say, it's all right if you don't ride like a cowboy," Quinn whispered. "They just need basic skills."

"I meant, I don't ride at all," Corey replied. "Like . . . never been on a horse. I grew up in New York City."

"Everyone in New York rides a horse!" Quinn shot back.

Which, Corey realized, was probably true. In 1917.

"Your family rich?" Quinn asked. "You only ride in automobiles?"

"Well, no to the first question," Corey said.

"And the second . . . ?"

Quinn was staring at him. His eyes were big, blue, and penetrating. Corey had the feeling he could smell a lie a mile away.

"Okay, I have a confession to make," Corey said quietly. "I'm not from around here. Well, I am, but I'm not. It's hard to explain. But it is super important that

I get back to where I need to go. The thing is, Quinn, I need something in order to do it. And what I need is either in the subway trench—the Gash—or in Haak's Pawnshop."

"Like, a ticket?"

"Like some coins. And a little rectangular metal thing that fits in your hand."

"That makes absolutely no sense."

"I know! Trust me, I'm leaving out the stuff that makes even less sense. But even if I *could* ride a horse, I couldn't be a West Side cowboy. Because I have to go."

"The cops didn't give us a choice, Corey. Look, it doesn't have to be so bad. I'll do the riding part of the job, and you do the other stuff. Meanwhile, maybe we can sneak some horse time. I can train you!"

Corey didn't know how to answer that. Living in 1917 with no income . . . searching for his stolen stuff . . . all of it would be super hard to do himself. So Quinn could really be a great help. But making friends would be dangerous. Corey would have to admit the truth at some point—and who would possibly believe some wack story about traveling from the twenty-first century? "Thanks. I'll do whatever the cops want. But afterward I have to be on my own."

Quinn raised an eyebrow. "You're a real pip."

"I know. Sorry."

"You're not telling me something important about yourself, are you?"

Corey looked away.

"That's okay," Quinn quickly added. "Maybe I'm not telling you something about myself either. I think you and me, we're birds of a feather. Both running away from something. But New York's a dangerous place, and there's strength in numbers. Look, you know the city, I know horses. We can help each other. The job with the cops will only last a day, because I'm going to be a West Side cowboy. And I want you to come with me. Let me tell you—riding a horse in front of a slow train? It's the world's easiest way to make money. All you gotta do is keep your balance. I can teach you. I can also help you get whatever was stolen from you. All you gotta do is be my friend and my guide to the city. If the plan fails, we go our own ways. Deal?"

Corey took a deep breath. This guy was the biggest noodge he'd ever met. And sometimes noodges made sense. "Deal."

Officer Blunt was trundling toward them with arms full of produce. "Nourishment for our new recruits!" he called out.

The two boys grabbed fruits from the cops and

began gobbling them down. "Hungry fellas, well, well!" Blunt said. "Eat up. You'll need the energy because you're starting work right now. Follow me!"

Corey nearly choked on his pear. "Wuurrfmm?" he blurted out, as Blunt grabbed his shoulder and pushed him toward the police station.

21

Corey wasn't sure if Speed Horse Stall Mucking was a rodeo event. But when Quinn managed to excavate a mountain of manure before Corey could muck out one stall, the entire precinct burst into applause.

Except for Blunt.

Quinn had bet the precinct captain that he could do the job in under a half hour. Amazingly, he'd won. Not so amazingly, the prize for winning was the use of a horse to train Corey.

Quinn's negotiating skills were impressive. But now Corey was on said horse. And he was fast becoming the afternoon comedy entertainment for New York's Finest.

"Ride high in the saddle!" Quinn shouted, looking

at Corey as if he were a space alien. *"High in the saddle!"*

"I d-d-don't even kn-kn-know what that m-m-means—*ow!*" Corey bit his tongue so hard he nearly fell off. For a moment the rafters of the stable seemed to go rubbery.

Riding was nothing like he expected. It looked so easy. Even Zenobia knew how to do it. But to Corey, it was like sitting on a jackhammer. He was already aching in places he'd never felt pain before. Through the door of the police stable, he heard the whistle of a freight train running up the far West Side. Just beyond it was the silver-blue expanse of the Hudson. He had a great urge to hop onto one or jump into the other.

Officer Blunt had promised this horse was gentle. But its name, Chaos, should have been a clue. All Corey was supposed to do was ride him in a wide circle. But Chaos was zigzagging around as if he were at a dance audition.

The police had all gathered off to the side of the stable. Some of them were doubled over with laughter. Tears rolled down Officer Blunt's sideburns.

"Take control!" Quinn shouted. "Show him who's boss!"

Corey pulled back on the reins. "Come on, Chaos!" he said desperately. "You're embarrassing me. Go right!"

Chaos snorted and went left, his eyes on a salt lick near the exit. Next to the salt lick were a few bales of hay. Corey noticed one of them twitch. A moment later, a giant rat emerged.

As the rodent scurried toward the open door, one of the cops began racing after it with a baseball bat. Chaos reared up and whinnied. And Corey fell over backward onto the dirt floor, landing on his behind.

"Well, that was successful," he said through a grimace.

Quinn raced over, grabbing Chaos's reins. "Whoa, easy, feller! Easy. That's my buddy you just threw. Go on. Apologize. Say you're sorry."

"He's . . . a horse!" Corey said, nearly choking on the blood of his bitten lip.

"Sometimes you gotta talk to them like babies," Quinn said, pulling a handkerchief from his jeans pocket. "Take this. Clean yourself up. You did great."

"I did?" Corey said.

"Well, you have potential." Quinn led Chaos to a hitching post by the door, tied him up, and then returned to Corey. "Tell me again, how is it you are alive and thirteen years old and you don't know how to ride a horse?"

"I prefer camels?" Corey said.

Before Quinn could answer, Officer Blunt announced, "Gentlemen, on your feet! We have us an extinguished visitor!"

The two boys stood. Officer Blunt stepped aside to reveal the skinniest man Corey had ever seen. His face looked like it had been chiseled in chalk and his body was bent like a parenthesis. A top hat was perched on his head, and he stared at Quinn through a set of smudged glasses perched at the end of a twiglike nose. When he spoke, his voice was like the creak of an old hinge. "How fortunate you boys happened to be here on my daily visit to the precinct." He walked toward Quinn with a sharp, appraising glance. "I am impressed by your ease with horses. Officer Blunt tells me you are a cowboy seeking employment."

"Two cowboys," Quinn corrected him. "Quinn Roper and Corey Fletcher at your service! I came all the way from Wyoming to answer your flyer. Corey here is from . . . Egypt. Once he gets the hang of horses, he'll be an expert!"

"Wait," Corey said. "No!"

"Pleased to meet you," the man said. "Randall Lyme."

He stuck out his hand. Shaking it was like squeezing eels and Corey quickly let go.

But Quinn pumped the old man's hands with great enthusiasm. "You're the guy on the flyer—R. Lyme! In the flesh! Pleased to meet you, sir!"

"Very well," Lyme croaked, "I will expect to see you tomorrow morning at seven for evaluation."

"We'll both be there!" Quinn said.

"Yes, well . . . ," Lyme said, casting a disapproving glance at Corey. "I trust things will work out. Otherwise I am sure Officer Blunt will have further duties commensurate with your skill level. Are we in agreement?"

"Oh, yes!" Quinn said.

"Baller," Corey drawled.

Mr. Lyme narrowed his eyes. "Excuse me?"

"That's Ancient Egyptian," Corey said, "for yee-hah."

Quinn was practically bouncing down Morton Street. Which was dangerous when there were people sleeping in shadows between the sidewalk's gas lamps. Saloons lined both sides of the block, and at 7:00 on a fall night, the bars were full. "What are you so excited about?" Corey asked.

"Our job!" Quinn shouted, nearly stomping on the head of an unconscious guy sprawled in the gutter.

"Yee-hah! Watch out, New York!"

"We don't have the job yet," Corey said. "We have to try out. Well, you do. They wouldn't hire me in a million years, unless they need a comic act."

"Maybe we'll get lucky tonight and find what was stolen from you," Quinn said. "Then, poof, you'll be gone. Back to . . . ?"

"Egypt," Corey said. "According to you."

"Ha! Sorry, first thing that popped into my head," Quinn replied. "Now look here, in case it takes a while to find your stolen goods, you'll need a job. Just give me one, maybe two hours to train you. They'll be begging you to be a West Side cowboy. You've got talent, Corey."

"How can you tell?" Corey said.

"I can tell things about people, things even they don't know. I've had practice." Quinn turned and started walking up the street again. "Come on, let's do this."

They went three steps before a man with a bloody forehead came running out of a brick building, followed by a woman brandishing a cast-iron skillet. A group of men barreled out of a bar, eyes on the chase like it was some kind of sports event, whooping and cheering at the top of their lungs. Corey pulled Quinn back, and they watched the couple disappear down the block.

Corey knew this street from the twenty-first century. He had taken music lessons from a teacher in this neighborhood. But the Village *he* knew had sleek glass condos, bright streets, traffic, and lots of people strolling to and from the river.

Now, it creeped him out.

They stayed to the middle of the street. There weren't many cars or horses at this hour, and as many people seemed to be walking in the street as on the sidewalk. In the upper windows of some buildings, children stared out listlessly. The tinkling sound of piano music spilled out from bar after bar, even from some apartment windows. At least five or six people were belting songs loudly and off key. A bored-looking old man gazed down from an apartment window and spilled foul-looking liquid onto the sidewalk. It splashed on the face of a sleeping drunk, who just smiled and turned to the other side.

"Guess we're not in Wyoming anymore, huh?" Corey said.

"The nightlife isn't so different out west," Quinn said, "just not so squashed together. Are you looking at the faces? Should we be peeking into the bars to find those two guys who robbed you?"

"I don't know," Corey said. "That's a lot of people, and I don't think they'll let me in at my age. Can we go back to the place where I woke up—you know, the Gash? There were two guys there who tried to help. I'm pretty sure I can recognize their faces. They gave me the thieves' names. Maybe they can help us find them."

"And if they give you any trouble . . ." Quinn pulled aside his leather vest, to reveal a holstered bowie knife.

Corey swallowed hard. "You don't really use that, do you?"

"Not unless I have to," Quinn said.

"That's reassuring," Corey replied, heading up the street.

In a couple of blocks, they reached the subway construction. At night the Gash was a thick strip of black stretching all the way up to Seventh Avenue and down to Varick Street. Pinpoints of candlelight flickered inside as people moved around like giant glowworms. Corey heard the strains of a banjo below and caught sight of a fire pit where an unidentified animal was being roasted on a stick. At each block, the dim reflection of the gas lamps from the cross streets cast a dull glow on the makeshift bridges.

Standing close to the edge and looking uptown, Corey had a sudden realization of where he was. "This is Seventh Avenue South . . . ," he murmured.

"They have a name for this disaster area?" Quinn said.

"Not yet, but they will," Corey said. "See that big street up north? That's Seventh Avenue. It used to end at Fourteenth Street, I guess. Couldn't extend any farther south because buildings were in the way—but those buildings were torn down to make the Gash and are gone forever. So once they put in the train, they'll cover the tunnel with a new street, and they'll need a name for it. But the address numbers on Seventh Avenue start at single digits and increase as you go uptown. You can't use negative numbers as addresses— minus-ten Seventh Avenue or whatever. So that's why they'll give the street a different name—Seventh Avenue South! Huh. Interesting. I always wondered about that."

Quinn scratched his head. "That's the kind of thing you find interesting?"

But Corey had his eyes on the flickering candles

below. Three of them were moving together. Lighting up a group of faces.

They were all men, bearded and smiling, their eyes fixed on Corey and Quinn. Lit from underneath, they looked ghoulish. Corey couldn't tell if they were young or old. "Fella, can you help a fallen pal?" one of them called out in a raspy voice. "It's my buddy Clarence here. He was up where you are, but he was in his cups and fell in. Can you see him? He's hurt pretty bad."

The guy was holding his candle away from himself now, trying to illuminate something—or someone—on the ground below.

Corey and Quinn walked closer, straining to see the outline of a man who let out a pitiful moan. "Maybe we should go back to the precinct house," Quinn suggested. "Get him some help."

Before Corey could answer, a kid dressed in loose clothes and a cap scurried up a ladder from inside the Gash, leaped onto the street, and grinned at both of them. "Have a nice trip," he said.

With a sudden, sharp jab, he shoved them in the chest, away from the dark trench.

Corey felt the underside of his legs hit against something hard. They gave out from under him and he tumbled backward, flying over the backs of two guys who had crouched on all fours behind them.

As Corey smacked to the ground, he took a kick to his head. He drew himself into a ball, but the kicks kept coming.

22

Corey couldn't see a thing. His head was tucked to his chest, his arms pulled tight around his face. But the boots landed hard on his back, his arms, his torso, his legs. He couldn't tell how many people had surrounded them but it felt like a hundred. He heard Quinn grunting, yelling.

Corey rolled away, lashing out with his arm. He fingers closed on someone's leg. The guy jumped away, but Corey clung to the pants and pulled as hard as he could.

"Yeeeaaagghh!" The attacker fell backward, wind-milling his arms, and crashed into the guy who was pummeling Quinn.

Both guys lost their balance, falling onto a pile of

sharp rocks. As they cried out in pain, Corey sprang toward Quinn and lifted him to his feet. His cowboy hat had fallen off and he quickly rammed it back down on his head.

"Let's get out of here!" Corey shouted.

The two fallen guys were crawling away, trailing blood. Quinn looked at them with disbelief. "You knock my hat off, you pay," he grunted. "Cowards."

The men were struggling to their feet. But Corey's eyes were drawn to a movement beyond him, in the shadows of the buildings.

Three other men stepped out. They didn't look much older than Quinn. Two of them had their hands behind their backs. They all wore ragged clothing and matching wool caps perched at the same slant. "Nobody does that to an ooga-ooga boy," said one of them, flashing a grin that revealed a set of teeth like piano keys.

"And no one calls us cowards," another said.

"The *who?*" Quinn howled with laughter. "That's the name of your gang—ooga-ooga? I take it back. You ain't cowards. You sound more like a species of monkey. And you look like it, too!"

The guy balled up his fists. As he lunged for Quinn, the two other guys stepped toward Corey. They were pulling their hands from behind their backs. One guy was an enormous seven footer holding a crowbar, the other a skinny rat-faced boy holding a broken wood plank.

Corey stepped backward, tripping over on a jagged rock. He nearly lost his balance, teetering at the edge of the trench.

"Jump!" shouted some drunk below, with a cackling laugh.

"Come home to daddy," another one growled.

"YAHHH!" One of the ooga-ooga boys ran for Corey with the crowbar held high. He took a wild swing.

Corey felt the whoosh of air as he jumped away, keeping the trench behind him. He scooped up a fistful of gravel and rocks, tossing it into the guy's face. The attacker flinched and turned away, hacking. Corey glanced quickly over to Quinn. He was spinning on his feet, landing a kick to the jaw of his assailant.

"Psst, kid, take this," a croaky voice called up from the trench.

Corey glanced down. In the darkness, a guy with a floppy, ripped cap and a scraggly beard was creeping up the ladder, reaching to Corey with an empty glass bottle. Corey had to fall to his belly to grab it.

The bottle smelled foul and was sticky to the touch. But it would have to do.

"Corey, watch out!" Quinn shouted.

Corey leaped to his feet, just in time to see the skinny ooga-ooga boy stepping toward him, drawing back with the plank.

He leaped away, scooped a rock from the ground with his free hand, and threw it. As the guy swung, the plank struck the rock with a loud *thock*, and the rock sailed over the trench and through the window of a building across the street. "Hey, grand slam!" Corey said. "Let's celebrate."

The weight of the plank had turned the guy's body around. Before he could recover, Corey jumped toward him and swung the bottle into the side of his face. It smashed to pieces, leaving Corey with a jagged stump in his hand. "I don't believe I just did that. . . ."

"Yee-HAH!" Quinn yelled, running toward him. "Nice work, Cor—"

The word caught in his throat. He stopped at Corey's side. The ooga-ooga boys were facing them in a line now, shoulder to shoulder—the crowbar guy, the plank guy with blood streaming down the right half of his face, and the guys who had fallen on the rocks. "Should we scrub 'em, Satch," growled the crowbar guy, "or just take their money?"

"Money first," said the guy who had started the

attacks. "Then, boys, we have us some fun."

Corey's hands were shaking. He held up the broken bottle. He could see a flicker of fear across their faces. Or maybe it was just his imagination.

"You're shaking, nelly boy," said the plank guy. "Maybe I need to make a line drive single out of your head."

Quinn stepped forward. Corey heard a soft *shhhhink* sound as he pulled the bowie knife from its holster. It glinted dully in the reflection of the gas lamp on the corner of Morton Street. "Not before I make a dugout in yours," he said.

"Quinn, be careful!" Corey hissed.

With a bloodthirsty yell, Satch grabbed the crowbar and swung it at Quinn. It connected with a thud to Quinn's wrist. His arm jerked backward and he cried out in pain.

"No-o-o-o!" Corey jumped at Satch, swinging the broken bottle. He felt it slice the guy's arm. Satch jumped back.

Quinn shifted the knife to his other hand, grimacing with pain. But as he looked toward Corey, his eyes grew as wide as softballs. "*Duck!*"

Corey squatted fast. He was aware of one of the ooga-ooga boys swinging something. And of Quinn lunging forward. And of a sickening groan.

Then everything fell silent.

"Quinn?" Corey said, still huddled in a crouch. "What just happened?"

Corey felt a drop of warm liquid land on the back of his neck. Quinn was backing away, still holding the knife, his arms at his sides. In the distance, a low, droning siren sounded.

"It's the police," one of the gang boys muttered.

Satch glowered at Quinn. "We don't forget," he growled, as the gang began slipping away into the shadows. Corey counted four of them.

The fifth was the plank guy. He was sprawled on the rocks, facedown in a pool of blood.

Quinn was standing over him, looking down at his inert body. Even in the darkness, Corey could see Quinn's face slowly going pale with shock over what he had just done.

23

After an entire Saturday of rehearsals, Leila was ready to scream. So she did. She walked into her room, kicked off her shoes, and let loose.

"Do you finally hate Stephen Sondheim?" her mom called from her office down the hall.

"Yee-e-es," Leila sang back.

"Happens to everyone!" she said. "But it's temporary."

It really, really helped to have a mom who understood.

Into the Woods was hard. Stephen Sondheim, the composer, was famous for writing hard music. Not to mention the staging, the lines, all of it—and Leila's part, the witch, was the toughest vocal role ever written. Right now her throat felt like it was punctured with holes. Plus Rachel had kept forgetting her lines. And even though Claudia's latest breakup had happened three weeks ago, she talked about it all through rehearsal and during the pizza party afterward, while eating every one of Leila's spinach and mushroom slices.

Arggh.

She fell back on her bed. At least all the work had kept her mind off Corey. Sort of.

For about the nine hundredth time that day, she checked her phone. Not a word. For about the thousandth time, she checked her actual brain memory for the status of Corey's grandmother, and it came back *dead*. Nothing about that had adjusted. Okay, okay, so she hadn't survived. But what about Corey? Her heart was doing flip-flops. There had to be a way to know what happened. Soon Corey's parents were going to suspect he wasn't having a sleepover. Maybe they knew already.

Maybe there was a way Leila could *know* what had happened to him. He was a part of history now. If he was trapped in the attack, his name would be listed among the victims.

Her fingers felt icy cold as she tapped "Corey Fletcher World Trade Tower" into her search bar. She felt like

217

throwing up as she tapped Enter. But his name wasn't there. Which gave her about three nanoseconds of relief, until she realized the flaw in her logic. *If he died, how would anyone know his name?*

He didn't work there, he was on no lists. Nobody would file a missing-persons report. He was a visitor from a different time.

She sat up and looked out her window, half expecting him to be walking up the street, whistling. In her mind he was eating a chocolate bar from the Mani Market on Columbus. It was his favorite thing to do.

The street was empty. But for the first time since entering the room, she noticed the lacquer box, still sitting on her desk.

Leila lifted it close, looking at the winter scene. The skaters looked so lifelike, so full of fun. They made her feel like she could just step in and join them. Maybe, if Corey survived and came home, he could teach her how to time travel back to this scene. Like a little tourist visit to the 1800s.

Now she felt tears pressing against her eyes. Was this what life was going to be like now? Always thinking about her best friend and knowing that he had gotten killed in the greatest disaster in American history?

Sadness and rage and heartache and frustration all

raced around inside her brain, colliding against each other, exploding to bits. Her teeth were grinding so hard her jaw hurt. With a cry of helplessness, she drew the lacquer box back and threw it. It flew end over end toward the pile of Auntie Flora's belongings by the door. With a loud crash, it smacked into the framed photo she had propped against the wall.

As the protective glass shattered into tiny shards, the box bounced back onto the floor. It left a big, ugly gash in the photo.

"*Leila?*" her mom cried out. She was in the hallway in an instant, pushing the door open to her room. "What the heck just happened?"

"An accident," Leila said. "I got carried away . . . practicing choreography. Big gestures, small room, bad choice."

"Wait, *what?*"

"Yeah, I'm an idiot. But no scratches. I'll clean it up. Really. You be sure to make your deadline."

Her mom gave her a dubious look, then backed out. "Maybe you need a nap, Leila. You don't sound like yourself."

As the door shut, Leila crouched down by the photo. It was the 1914 gathering of the Knickerbockers, only now the heads of four members in the back row had been bashed in, replaced by a hole. She reached behind the image. The cardboard backing had been punctured, too. She pressed it in, but it would need a professional to restore it to its former glory. With a sigh, she shook loose as much of the glass as she could.

That was when she noticed the enormous white cat at the bottom right of the photo.

At first glance she'd thought it was a polar bear. But at this distance it was definitely alive and very feline. As she looked closer, she noticed the doglike snout, the piercing eyes.

"Catsquatch . . . ," she murmured.

The resemblance was uncanny. Leila set the photo down against the wall again. She knew she had to get a broom and a dustpan, but she couldn't take her eyes from the cat. It looked so . . . present. So alive and intelligent. Just like its modern-day version.

She stood and backed away, inadvertently kicking the box. As she bent down to pick it up, it still felt weirdly warm to the touch. Holding it in her hand, she examined the outside, turning the box 360 degrees. Up close, she could see the finely ornamented brass hasp that kept the box shut. It was an octagonal shape, with a round keypad in the center that showed the numbers 1 to 6 next to six small black buttons.

But Leila couldn't keep her eyes from the photo. The white cat seemed to be growing brighter. For a moment Leila imagined that its paw was raised.

No. Her imagination was playing tricks. She was thinking about the real Catsquatch, earlier that day. The way it had followed her and Rachel, like it had something important to say. The way it had raised its paw and tapped it down repeatedly on the sidewalk like a horse in a circus.

Four . . . three . . . five . . . two . . .

Leila felt the blood flush from her veins. She sat on the bed, clutching the box, glancing at the photo.

What if it was trying to say something?

The idea seemed ridiculous. Impossible.

But so did time travel.

Her fingers shaking, she pressed the buttons in order. Four. Three. Five. Two.

The hasp snapped open. Placing her hand on the lid, Leila opened it carefully and looked inside.

24

Corey helped Quinn down into the trench. The tough Wyoming cowboy was in tears as he landed on the dirt floor. Above them, the fallen ooga-ooga boy's boots jutted out over the rim of the wall. "I—I didn't mean to do that," Quinn said.

"You saved our lives," Corey replied.

All along the Gash, people were scrabbling up various ladders to the top, trying to peek over to see the body. "He got Ratboy . . . ," someone called out breathlessly.

"Get outta here," another voice answered.

A long, low whistle. "There's gonna be blood for that."

Corey felt a poke in his back and spun around to see

the man who had handed him the empty bottle. "Take this," he said, thrusting a lit kerosene lamp toward him. "Name's Okun. Wally Okun. Head downtown, kid. You and your friend get out of the neighborhood. You heard the siren, right? Well, notice the cops ain't here yet? Surprise, surprise, they're always slow when it comes to protecting the Gash. Lots of noise but no action. They'd rather see us kill each other off. So this gives you some time, but not enough for tea and crumpets, if you catch my drift. If they see you, you're outta luck. And that's the least of your problems."

Quinn was gazing upward, shaking his head in shock. "I killed a man."

"That's right, kid," Okun said, "but I saw it. It was self-defense. He woulda killed you without blinking an eye."

"They'll catch me," Quinn went on, "and they'll send me home. That can't happen. I can't go home. . . ."

"We have to go, Quinn." Corey put a hand on his shoulder, then turned to the kind stranger. "Thanks, Mr. Okun. How will I get the lamp back to you?"

"Don't worry about it." Okun's face was taut with urgency. His features were sunken and dirty, but his back was straight and he stood close to seven feet tall. "Do exactly as I say. Walk fast. Anyone tries to bother you along the way, tell them the Commander sent you. Everybody respects me down here. Climb out of here at Varick Street and walk east. Lay low for the night in some rooming house in the Bowery, where you don't have to give a name. By tomorrow everything will be hunky-dory."

Behind him a group of about a dozen had formed. They were muttering *amens* and *you bets*.

One of the Gash people who had climbed up to the surface was now coming back down. "Hey, cowboy, the guy you slit—he's still breathing. I'd get outta here pronto if I was you."

Quinn looked relieved, but the small crowd did something Corey hadn't expected. They burst into catcalls and nasty sound effects.

"Shoulda been offed . . ."

"Woulda served him right . . ."

"Animals . . ."

"We don't like the gangs," Okun explained, talking fast. "Things is bad enough down here with the rummies and rats, but we try to keep peaceful. We watch out for our own and know each other's business. Like family. We ain't angels, but we don't stab and shoot. To them gangs, human life don't mean nothing."

Corey glanced around, hoping to see the faces of the two drunken guys he'd first met in the Gash, but it was hard to make out features in the darkness. "Help me, Mr. Okun, before we go. I fell in here myself this afternoon. When I woke up, my money and some personal stuff were gone from my pocket. We went to Haak's Pawnshop—"

"Filcher take you there?" Okun broke in.

"How did you know?" Corey said.

"The snake," Okun spat, shaking his head. "Those two got a racket, Filcher and Haak. Filcher pays guys to fleece the unconscious souls down here—of which there are many—and then they fork over the goods to him for payment. Sometimes they double-cross him and pawn the goods to Haak instead—but Filcher has his ways of getting his cut."

"We know," Corey said. "Hey, do you guys know anybody named Hans and Benny-boy?"

Okun looked over his shoulder. A mob of curious Gash people had gathered behind him. "You ain't got time for chitchat—"

"We heard they were the ones who took my stuff," Corey barreled on.

"Yeah? Well, them two both died months ago.

Whoever told you that was their names—they was lying." Okun turned and called into the crowd: "Any of youse seen who fleeced this nice kid?"

A murmur went through the crowd. After a moment voices began piping up:

"Coulda been Knuckles . . ."

"Knuckles is dead, ya numbskull . . ."

"No he ain't!"

"Or Sammy the Clam . . ."

"Big Doogie . . ."

"Li'l Schmutzie . . ."

"How do we know this kid is tellin' the truth?"

"He can go back to his mommy and daddy for money. . . ."

"Leave some of that money wit' us!"

This was useless. In the distance, Corey could hear voices yodeling "Ooga-*oooooga!*" At the sound, the crowd fell into an instant silence.

Okun exhaled hard. He began pushing Corey and Quinn south. "That shout—it means the gang is calling for reinforcements. They'll gather in the shadows and wait for the cops to come here. After the cops leave, they'll move in. That's how they work. Now *go!* And watch your backs."

"What about you guys?" Quinn asked.

"They know enough not to bother us anymore," Okun said with a cocky grin. "They'll be looking for youse."

Corey could hear a distant clopping of horse hooves. Without another word, he pointed the kerosene lamp downtown. The Gash people, little more than silhouettes, parted to the sides of the trench.

Quinn mouthed a quick *thanks* to Okun, and the two boys began to run.

Corey knew that warm air rose, but nothing proved it better than the top floor of a Bowery flophouse. After the six-floor climb, his entire body was covered with sweat that felt like hot glue.

The Bowery was a neighborhood that made the Gash seem upscale. The filth on the sidewalks crept up your ankles as you walked. Here, the down-and-outers slept on hot cement sidewalks, on cardboard boxes and piles of rags. They slept through the clatter of the elevated train. Soot-stained tenement buildings lined both sides of the street, most of them with hand-drawn Vacancy signs, usually followed by words like LOWEST RATES! or CHEAP!

That last part seemed about perfect for Corey's and Quinn's purposes.

The Better Ridgefield Hotel sounded promising. But half the steps were missing, the walls had fist-size holes, and the stink of body odor and rotten food seemed to be at war. As a distraction, Corey went over in his mind the list of names he'd heard in the Gash: *Knuckles, Sammy the Clam, Big Doogie, Li'l Schmutzie.* He would have to start gathering info on these guys as soon as he could. In the meantime he and Quinn needed to lie low from the ooga-ooga boys. This place was cheap enough, and it would just have to do.

As he pushed open the door to their room, Corey saw the advantages to sleeping on the sidewalk. The room smelled awful. The walls were grayish-black but looked suspiciously like they'd been painted white during the Jurassic era. It was just large enough for one ratty-looking bed and a rickety table with a metal chair. The only window faced an airshaft. Across the shaft was another window into another room, where a sunken-faced, bare-chested old man was asleep and snoring on a sofa.

"If this is the Better Ridgefield Hotel," Corey said, "what's the less-good Ridgefield Hotel like?"

"They told us it was the presidential suite!" As Quinn's eyes scanned the squalid room, he looked agitated and jumpy. "I thought there might be two rooms.

You know, one for each."

"Some tough cowboy," Corey said. "We'll make the best of it. Tomorrow morning we head to the Hudson River, where I humiliate myself and you get a great job. Then we can live in style. After you get paid." He flopped down onto the bed, which sent up a cloud of dust. A small squadron of insects scurried out from under the mattress and ran for the corner.

Quinn let out a noise between a shout and a squeak. "What in blazes are those?"

"Cockroaches," Corey said, trying to sound braver than he felt.

"Do they bite?"

"Nah. They're the official mascot of New York City."

Quinn swallowed hard. "We could try sleeping in Central Park."

"It's like four miles away. And it has rats. Those do bite." Corey felt his eyes closing. "Aren't you tired?"

"No." Quinn pulled the chair to the other side of the room and swung it around so it faced the door. "You go ahead. I—I don't think it's . . . safe for us both to be asleep at the same time."

Corey yawned. The sheets seemed surprisingly clean, so he took off his sweaty shirt and fell back on the bed. "Dude, you don't sound like yourself."

"What do you mean?"

"You were like a superhero with those thugs. You stood up to Satch. And the plank guy. Now you're all jumpy."

"Yeah. Well . . ."

Quinn's face was turning red, and Corey felt a pang of guilt. What was the point of making fun of a guy who had just saved his life? "I guess you got kind of spooked, when you thought you killed that guy," he said gently.

Quinn nodded. "I guess."

"Sorry, Quinn, you're my hero. Maybe you can lasso some cockroaches while I snooze. I'll get up soon, and we can take"—Corey let out a big yawn—"tunes. . . ."

"Huh?"

"Turns," Corey corrected himself.

As he drifted off to sleep, Quinn was sitting bolt upright in his chair, facing the other way. He was scribbling something in a small leather-bound book. Corey had no idea where he'd kept that hidden, or what he was writing.

Maybe cowboy poetry.

Corey smiled. To each his own.

25

Leila stared cautiously into the lacquer box. She pulled out thirteen foreign coins, two lockets, and four necklaces. A flip phone with a Post-it note that said *Recycle this!* A feather. A fountain pen. A nail file. A faded pin that said WOODSTOCK '69. A framed selfie of Auntie Flora in a crowd, most likely Times Square, her "home away from home." At the very bottom was a leather book.

That was all.

Leila sighed, placing the book back into the box. This wasn't what she'd expected. Not after the last twenty-four hours, when her best friend had gotten stuck in time and a monster cat had revealed the secret combination to this box. Leila had been stoked for finding something *crazy*—maybe a smoldering gun-powder pellet or a tiny mouse king puffing on a tiny mouse pipe. But these were ordinary Auntie Flora–type souvenirs.

Leila took a deep breath. She was jittery. She was finding weirdness in normal things. Maybe the cat hadn't tapped out a combination. Maybe it was a coincidence. Or maybe the lock would have yielded to any random combo. The box may have been made with a wood that absorbed warmth naturally. And the white cat in the old photo may just have been . . . a white cat in an old photo.

Rachel was texting her now. If anybody could be counted on to do that at the wrong time, it was Rachel. Leila quickly checked: it was a small flurry of apologies about the rehearsals, with lots of sad emojis. Leila was in no mood for that.

Instead of answering, she reached into the box and pulled out the leather book that lay at the bottom. It was a beautiful journal, bound by a loosely knotted silk ribbon and labeled with her aunt's initials, AFS, Augusta Flora Sharp.

As Leila picked it up, the ribbon slipped loose. The leather cover was scorched in one spot but otherwise soft and nubbly, with a pattern of intertwined branches

around the border. The rough-cut paper edges felt
feathery. Claudia and Rachel thought Leila was crazy
for loving the smell of books, but here in private she
could yank open the journal and inhale. The pages
didn't seem like paper at all, more like linen, with fine
grains and imperfections. She wanted to run her fingers over a page, but she felt funny looking at Auntie
Flora's private thoughts. Those were none of her business. So she turned to find a blank page.

Shreds of paper rained out of the book.

The very last three pages were scratched and cut up
into strips that barely hung together. As if Auntie Flora
had transformed into a toddler with a pair of scissors.

Leila flipped back a few pages, all ripped. Finally
she reached the journal's last entry. There, the handwriting was jagged and primitive looking, not at all
like Auntie Flora's neat, organized script:

don't know if I can keep up this charade any longer. It's
not fair to dear, sweet, patient Lazslo. I have tried
so hard. But Gus was right. It is possible to become
addicted. It's happened to me.

He said you will begin to NEED the experience.
And no matter how many times they warn you of the

> consequences, you never think it will happen to you.
> But I feel it. And I don't know how much longer I'll be
> myself. . . .

Leila sat down on her bed. Her head felt light.

Auntie Flora was one of them. A time-hopper, or whatever you called them.

She'd always been theatrical and moody, but she'd become a little strange and distant lately. Now Leila knew why. Flora was OD'ing on time travel. Becoming addicted. Papou had warned Corey about that sort of thing.

One by one, the people Leila really liked were disappearing. But why Auntie Flora? She stared again at the journal:

> I thought I could tough it out. I never imagined
> I'd be writing this. But I feel the change coming on.
> I dread I will not be able to fend it off. Fenton,
> Roseanne, Cosmo—they were all stronger people than
> I, but look what happened to them. The change took
> them lock, stock, and barrel. I cannot let Lazslo see
> me. I must suffer the throes of TS on my own. I can
> feel it happening as I wr

That was it. Nothing more. On the next page, the slashed pages began.

Why?

Leila's eyes scanned the page again. *The change . . . the throes of TS . . .* What change? What was TS? And who were those people—*Fenton, Roseanne, Cosmo . . . ?*

She began rifling back through the journal. Right away she knew it wasn't an ordinary diary. Page after page was full of notes from her Knickerbockers meetings. Discussions about clothes to wear to visit the Great Depression. Excited passages about trips to "pre-Colonial New Amsterdam." Musings about whether to try for a voyage on the *Titanic*.

I simply cannot keep myself from these trips. . . .

How much longer will Lazslo believe I am away on business. . . .

It pains me to have refrained from time travel these last four weeks. . . .

L. called the bureau in Mumbai and they told him I was at no such meeting. . . .

Dear, dear Cosmo deSmiglia has transspeciated. He fought the addiction. He hadn't hopped in a year. I suppose he backslid. I am told that now he is some hideous species of peccary. Things are not going well. . . .

Leila closed the book, numb.

Transspeciated . . . TS. Had to be the same thing.

And that name . . . deSmiglia.

Yesterday, when Leila had chased after Corey in the park, she had seen something on the way. That strange massive mutant rat. It had scared her to death. But when she brought it up, Papou had answered her:

"Ah, you met Smig."

Which sounded like deSmiglia.

Leila stared at the passage in the journal: *I am told that now he is some hideous species of peccary.* She quickly looked up the term "peccary" on her phone. In a second she was staring at the image of a hairy beast that resembled a warthog.

She placed the phone on her bed, her fingers shaking.

Smig had been "addicted." And so had Auntie Flora. But not to any controlled substance.

To time travel.

From outside, Leila heard a plaintive scream, like a child in bitter pain. Thinking it was a neighbor, she ignored it. But the wail grew louder and louder. And it sounded spookily like her name.

"Laaaaaaay . . . laahhhh . . ."

She ran to her window, threw it open, and looked down.

A couple was walking down the street, pushing a

stroller. A helmeted delivery guy was returning to his bike after dropping off a meal.

Leila almost missed seeing the lump of white, half-hidden by the plantings directly below. But as it slinked to the center of the sidewalk, Leila recognized it right away.

Catsquatch sat back on its haunches and raised its paw.

Leila could swear it was grinning.

26

Leila didn't usually go into Central Park alone after dark. But by the time she got to the sidewalk, Catsquatch was across the street, waiting in the park entrance.

She hurried across Central Park West and followed the white fluff into the park. The cat beast strutted along the pathway toward the reservoir, drawing the attention of a pit bull on a tight leash. With a horrible snarl, the dog lunged toward the big cat, teeth bared.

"*Is that thing yours?*" bellowed the dog's owner. He was a huge guy with tat-covered arms, but it took all his strength to restrain his pet. "*Get it away!*"

Before Leila could answer, Catsquatch turned to the pit bull and growled.

The dog jerked its head from side to side, foaming at the mouth. It sprang forward on its massive hind legs. The leash slipped out of the owner's hand. *"Masher, no!"*

But Catsquatch faced the dog head-on. The hair rose along the monster cat's spine. It sat back calmly on its haunches, then rose on its hind legs. Its eyes bugged, its fur spiked outward, and its claws sprang like knives. With a deep-throated hiss, it slashed the dog's snout.

The dog jumped back, falling to the pavement. With a low, guttural growl, Catsquatch began moving toward Masher, lumbering on its hind legs like an angry bear.

Masher scrambled to his feet. Whimpering, he circled around behind his owner. The man stared in disbelief. "What the heck *is* that?"

"A do-o-o-og's . . . wuhst . . . dweeeam," whispered a scratchy voice.

Leila whirled around to see who had spoken. She saw another dog walker with a very scared-looking Chihuahua, a jogger, a kid on a skateboard, and a couple arm in arm. But they were nowhere near enough.

Masher was pulling his owner away, but the guy was smirking at Leila. "Yeah, right. Funny voice. Hey, you got lucky. I don't know what spooked him. Must've been something he ate. Normally he destroys cats."

"I—I didn't say anything . . . ," Leila said, as the

guy and his dog vanished into the night.

Catsquatch was walking on all fours again, tail sashaying from side to side. As it pranced across the park's main road, it gave Leila a beckoning look over its shoulder. Then it disappeared into a thicket of bushes.

It was hard to find areas of Central Park that were not illuminated by overhead streetlights. But Catsquatch had managed. Carefully Leila crossed the road, ducked under low-hanging tree branches, and stepped into a tiny clearing.

Snuggled against the base of a tree, Catsquatch let out a sound between a purr and a growl. "We-e-ell, that was amusing, dahling, wasn't it?"

Leila screamed. She stumbled backward, twisting her ankle on an exposed root. Grimacing, she sank against the trunk of a maple tree as the big white cat began licking her ankle.

Only one person in the world called her *dahling*. "You—you're Auntie F-F-F—"

"Thank you. Thank you *so much* for not calling me by that howwid other name," the cat said. "An old gal still has a bit of pwide. You have no idea how lovely it is to speak English again. As you can see, I'm not vewy good yet. Especially the . . . lettah that comes between *q* and *s*."

"R?" Leila said.

"Pwecisely. Honestly, I don't know how Smig does it."

Breathe . . . breathe . . .

This could not be happening. Leila felt the world swirling around her. She wanted desperately to be dreaming. She closed her eyes tight and opened them again. But the ankle still hurt, the tree was against her back, and her aunt was a white cat beast. Everything was solid and real. "So . . . your journal . . . ," Leila said. "That stuff about t-t-trans . . . species . . ."

"Twansspeciating," Auntie Flora said.

"That. It happened to you, didn't it? From too much time travel—it adjusted your genes?"

Auntie Flora let out a satisfied purr. "Oh, mah-velous! You must have spoken to Gus. I was hoping he would explain the pwocess. I nevuh was able to let him know my . . . news. It was all so fast. Please tell him."

"If you can talk, why didn't you just tell *me*?" Leila asked. "I mean, all those times we saw you on the side-walk . . . ?"

"Well, deawy, I couldn't vewy well weveal myself to yo' fwiends!" Auntie Flora snapped.

"But you—you . . . ," Leila stammered.

Her aunt's exclamation hung in the air. Whatever

Leila was about to say was wiped out of her brain by an uncontrollable urge to laugh. All the pressure seemed to whoosh out of her like a burst balloon. She tried to choke it back but it came out in a big, loud guffaw.

"I know . . . I know . . . I sound widiculous . . . ," Auntie Flora said.

Now Leila was collapsing to the ground, gasping. "Oh! Oh! Sorry . . . sorry . . . it's just . . . you sound like yourself, but . . ."

"I look widiculous."

"No! I didn't mean that!"

Her aunt was turning away. "I will let you calm down."

"No! Don't go!" Leila leaned forward, scooping up the ungainly cat from the ground, hugging her. "I'm so sorry. It's just that I feel like I've been turned upside down these last twenty-four hours. Like a big night-mare. I love you, Auntie Flora. It's just . . . well, a lot for me to get used to."

"How do you think I feel?" her aunt said.

Leila sighed. "I know, I know. I shouldn't complain. You're the one who's suffering."

Auntie Flora's resistance was melting now. Her new body unstiffened. Leila sat there with her aunt, rock-ing her back and forth silently. Joggers thumped by them on the way to and from the reservoir. One or two gave them a startled glance, but Leila didn't care. "Does Uncle Lazslo know what happened?"

"No," Auntie Flora said. "I'm afwaid he wouldn't unduhstand."

"Corey's grandfather went to Vancouver because he heard there was a cure," Leila said. "Can I bring you to him? Maybe he can take you there, too."

Auntie Flora turned her big face up to Leila. Her eyes were piercing and very human. "Oh, please do, dahling. A cure? Weally? I hope so."

"Corey, too. He can do it, you know—time-hop."

"I know," Auntie Flora said. "I saw Smig. He was cagey but I got him to open up. I would love to see Cowwey. He won't need a cure if he sees what it did to me. He'll be wisah than I was."

Leila exhaled. "Corey is gone, Auntie Flora. He went back to 2001 to try to save his grandmother."

"Oh . . . ," Auntie Flora said, shrinking back. "Oh, how foolish. Didn't his gwandfatha tell him he can't change the events of—"

"He can," Leila interrupted. "He's a Throwback."

Her feline aunt leaped out of Leila's arms. "Impossible."

"No. It's like one in a million, but not impossible.

He's done it already, Auntie Flora—changed something in the past."

Auntie Flora began pacing back and forth. "Oh my . . ."

"I haven't heard from him. His grandmother is not alive. I'm worried."

"Of course you aw, dahling. Listen to me. Go back to my collection. I have a lacquew box that contains vewy impowtant things you'll need."

"The box! I've seen it! I thought the stuff inside was junk."

"Not junk. Awtifacts I've used to twavel in time. Nine-eleven is a pwized time destination for time-hoppers. It's kind of sick, I know. Evewyone seems to have an awtifact from 2001. Look for the small nail file in the lacquew box. It belonged to a Stuyvesant High School student who fled the attack."

"Wait. You want me to bring you the nail file so you can time-hop?" Leila shook her head. "In your condition?"

"Not me," Auntie Flora said. "You."

"But—I can't," Leila protested. "I—I'm not—"

"I have nevuh known you to lack self-confidence, Leila."

"I don't! I mean, about schoolwork and stuff like that. But—"

"We are blood welatives," Auntie Flora said. "This ability is passed down genetically. There is a chance you can do this. Not a huge chance, but there is one way to know. Pick up that nail file. If the file becomes hot to the touch, we have something."

"It *was* hot!" Leila said, bolting to her feet.

"The file?" Auntie Flora said.

"The whole box."

A cat's face did not show the emotion that a human's did, but Leila could swear Auntie Flora was smiling. "Take me to your woom," she said. "Now."

27

Quinn didn't respond the first time his name was called.

Holding a clipboard, a sour-faced man with stringy hair stood in front of a rowdy group of young men. In answer to the ad for West Side cowboys, they had all come to the makeshift metal hut near the Hudson River.

"Ahem. I repeat—number seven—Roper! Quinn Roper!" The man's nasal voice rang out.

Corey elbowed Quinn, who was slumped against the back of a stiff wooden chair, fast asleep. "That's you," Corey whispered.

"Wha— Huh—?" Quinn said.

"They called your name," Corey said. "Your turn."

They were both exhausted from the night at the Better Ridgefield Hotel. Corey didn't know which was worse—the bug-infested horsehair mattress he'd slept on, or the metal chair from which Quinn had not moved all night. Now, at seven in the morning, they were jammed together with dozens of men in a tin hut. Although the entrance was open to the river, Corey couldn't even feel a hint of a breeze.

Two rows in front of them, a smirking, skinny guy turned to his neighbor and said, "Watch this." He popped up from his seat and began strutting toward the front. "Yup—I'm Roper! That'll be me!"

Instantly awake, Quinn leaped to his feet. "No, you ain't."

He unhooked the rope from his shoulder. As he twirled it over his head, the man sitting next to him ducked away. Quinn sent the lasso flying over the heads of the other men. It fell around the skinny guy, pinning his arms to his sides. "What the devil?" he shouted.

"Follow me," Quinn said to Corey. Stepping quickly into the aisle, he yanked on the rope. As the hapless impostor fell to the floor, a cheer went up from the room.

"Excuse me . . . excuse me . . . ," Corey said, stepping over the other men as he tried to follow Quinn.

"*Git along, li'l dogie!*" Quinn shouted, dragging the

startled man toward him up the aisle floor. Now everyone in the room was standing. The guy was kicking and screaming as Quinn yanked him to his feet. Pulling the guy's face close, Quinn growled, "Don't. You. Ever. Do. That. Again."

With easy, quick moves, he untied the guy, coiled the rope back up around his shoulder, and strode to the front of the room. "Here I am, sir!"

The place exploded with laughter and whoops. Guys crowded the aisles to pat Quinn on the back. Chairs fell to the floor. In front, the guy with the clipboard began banging a hammer on a desktop. "Order! *Order!*"

Corey fought his way through the excited throng. As he and Quinn got to the front, the leader had to shout to be heard over the din. "Well, that sure was a humdinger." He offered Quinn a bony hand. "Name's Jensen."

"Roper," Quinn said. "This here's my best friend, Fletch. We come as a pair."

"A *pair?*" Corey said.

Quinn elbowed him in the side.

"I hire person by person," Jensen said. "Not pair by pair."

"We can split the fee," Quinn said with a shrug. "Either that, or we both walk, and you lose the best, bravest, and most reliable men here."

Jensen gave them each a long, appraising look. "Well, ya made me laugh. No one makes me laugh in the morning. Guess that oughtta be good for something. Follow me. But remember, if ya can't ride, ya lose the job."

Jensen led Quinn and Corey out the door. He walked with a noticeable limp, grabbing a cane that was propped by the entrance.

"What did you just do?" Corey whispered.

"Saved your butt," Quinn said.

They walked along the river's edge, heading south. As the din of the metal hut faded away, Corey could hear delighted screams coming from the water. Just ahead, a ladder led down to a small, lopsided dock that looked like it hadn't been used by boats in years. There, a group of boys were skinny-dipping in the river, their clothes in piles on the dock. One of them spotted Corey and waved. "Water's nice and cold!" he said. "Come on down!"

After the humid, showerless night at the Better Ridgefield Hotel, Corey was tempted. It sure would be a heck of a lot more fun than trying to ride a horse. "Later!" he called down.

Quinn and Jensen were heading away from the river, up a small hill toward the freight rail. Corey ran to catch up. Near the tracks was a small horse pen and stable. Behind that was a ten-story factory building. In present times, Corey thought, the factory would be barely noticeable. Here, it overwhelmed the landscape.

"The rail's pretty quiet at this hour," Jensen said. "But soon the train cars'll be chugging along. They run uptown, picking up meat from the shops on Gansevoort, then all kinds of goods from the shipyards in midtown. Then up the West Side to the Bronx, Yonkers, and Westchester. Goes on all day and through the night, every day. But this area here—this is where we have the safety problems. You'd think people would be smart enough to stay off the tracks, hah! Some of the drunks, they see track bed and they want to put a pillow in it and snooze!"

He thought his joke was so funny, he started wheezing with laughter. "Ya get that? Track bed . . . pillow? Hee! Anyways, someday they're gonna build an elevated track, if they can work out the politics. So for the time being, we need guys like you. Your job is to ride the horses in front of the trains and clear the tracks. Go too fast, and something could slip onto the tracks behind you. Go too slow, that train sneaks up faster'n you think, and your horse gets killed. Or you. Okay, wait here. I'll choose suitable steeds, one for each of you."

"No need to choose." As Quinn eyed the horses, he put his hand gently on the guy's shoulder. "I'll take the roan. Corey will like the chestnut."

Jensen gave him a curious but strangely impressed look. "Oh? The chestnut is new. He's still a little meek."

"We'll take him anyway." Quinn shrugged. "Hey, just saving you the headache of picking the right ones."

"All righty—Thunder and Paisley it'll be, then," Jensen replied, turning toward the pen.

Corey gave Quinn a look. "I hope Thunder's for you," he said.

"Yup." Quinn smiled. "Paisley will be as obedient as a mouse. Trust me. I know how to pick 'em."

Corey didn't trust horses. He was afraid Paisley would wander to the dock, dive in, and swim to New Jersey. That would be just his luck.

But Quinn had been right about this one. Paisley was easy to ride and agreeable.

Their test: trot down a siding, and make sure to clear it as efficiently as possible. Corey quickly learned that a "siding" meant a section of track that went nowhere—it led off to the side, kind of a parking area for trains. Jensen and his men had booby-trapped the rails with life-size dummies, branches, tree trunks, a car tire or two, and a baby carriage. Quinn was a natural, positioning himself just right and using a lasso. He was the one clearing almost all the debris. By the end of the test period, a crowd of bystanders from the neighborhood had gathered to watch.

Corey had a long broom handle. He did manage to push away at least four items. Luckily, none of the bystanders was looking at him.

After it was over, his legs felt wobbly from the riding. The temperature had shot up and the humidity made every inch of fabric stick to him. As he and Quinn dismounted, Jensen's only comment was, "You're hired. Report here for the late shift at five o'clock."

"Both of us?" Quinn said.

Jensen gave him a sour look. "You said that's the only way you'd do the job, right?"

It wasn't exactly a compliment, but Corey would take it.

"Thank you, sir!" Quinn said with a deep bow.

As the old guy limped back to the hut, Corey leaped into the air. "Woo-HOO!"

He threw his arms around Quinn. But instead of hugging him back, Quinn pushed himself away. "Woo-hoo?" he said.

"That's East Coast for *yee-hah*," Corey said. "Sorry, dude. I guess hugging isn't what guys do in Wyoming. In 1917. Whatever. But this is so awesome, Quinn! You taught me how to ride a horse."

Quinn nodded. His face was red. "Well. You're . . . awesome, too," he said. "Dude."

Corey could hear squeals and splashing from beyond the pilings that lined the river. "Now that we're free for a while, I have an idea," he said. "Follow me."

He ran toward the river and looked over. The group of swimmers had grown. There were maybe twelve of them, half wearing shorts and the other half skinny-dipping. It looked like some of them were brothers. Corey figured their ages were maybe eight to fourteen or so. Everyone looked cool and wet and happy. "Come on down!" a boy called upward.

"No grown-ups here!" another yelled. "So don't worry about being caught!"

"Twist our arms," Corey said, turning to climb down.

Quinn stepped to the edge and looked over. Eyes widening, he stepped back. "Nah. I'll pass."

"Oh . . . ," Corey said with sudden understanding. "You can't swim?"

"I can swim," Quinn replied. "I just don't want to."

The coolness of the river breeze felt great on Corey's back. He was dying to jump in. "Dude, we were in the Gash, and then that fleabag hotel. We didn't shower. You didn't even sleep. Plus, we just spent the morning on horses, I smell like a sewer, and the Hudson's not polluted like it's going to be in a few years. So the water will be awesome—"

"I said no," Quinn snapped. "Do what you want. I'll do what I want."

"'Smatter?" one of the kids yelled up. "Ya friend too good for us?"

As Quinn turned to go, one of the boys scrambled up the ladder, darting around Corey. The kid was quick and slippery, and he reached over the piling, pulling Quinn by the ankle.

Quinn was caught off guard. Windmilling his arms, he teetered backward and tumbled over the dock. Corey watched as he arced through the air and splashed into the river.

The boy on the ladder did a backflip after him, and his friends screamed with approval. Corey scrambled down the ladder. By the time he got to the rickety dock, Quinn had emerged, gasping for air and treading water. His hat had come off and gone floating away, but the boy who'd pulled him into the river grabbed it. Smashing it down on his own head, he shouted, "Yippie-ay-oh-ki-yay!"

Lunging through the water, Quinn took his hat back. With his other hand he grabbed the boy by the neck. "Nobody does that to me," he shouted, jerking his neck forward.

He butted his forehead sharply with the kid's, who sank back into the water. "Aaaaaay, whadja do that for?" one of the other boys shouted. "It was just a joke!"

With powerful strokes, Quinn swam to the dock. Corey kneeled, extending a hand to help. "Are you okay?" he asked.

Quinn's face was red. Clasping Corey's hand, he yanked him off the dock. "Are you?" he shouted, as Corey plunged in.

Now the other boys were hollering again. Corey felt the heaviness of his clothes weighing him down. He swam to the piling and pulled himself up. Quinn had made it to the ladder and was climbing fast, water cascading from his clothes.

"Wait!" Corey said, struggling to his feet.

By the time Corey got to the top of the ladder,

Quinn was striding angrily downtown. His wet boots crunched against the rocky soil. Corey ran after him as quickly as he could. "Quinn, sorry!" he shouted.

Quinn spun around. The brim of his waterlogged cowboy hat drooped on both sides like a bonnet, but the expression on his face was no laughing matter. "That's the thanks I get, huh?" he spat. "Just pull me into the water fully dressed in the only clothes I own, after I said no?"

"That wasn't me, Quinn," Corey replied. "It was one of those kids. And what was the big deal, anyway? It's just water. Your clothes will dry."

Quinn's face was red. "You egged them on. Because why? Because my no doesn't mean anything? Because you know what I want, better than I do?"

"Whoa, I never said that!" Corey protested.

"You know why I left Wyoming? Do you? It's because everybody knew the best for me. How I should dress, what I should believe, who I should make friends with, what I should be interested in. I thought people were different here. Obviously I was wrong."

"Dude, look, I know that sucked, okay? Those kids were jerks. But I didn't mean to diss you. If you'd told me how you felt about stuff like this, I never would have even considered—"

"*I don't have to tell you anything!*" Quinn shoved Corey hard. He stumbled backward and fell onto a sharp rock. Pain jolted up his body, taking his breath away. His vision blurred.

Quinn was standing over him now. Corey blinked away the pain. Mustering his strength, he tucked his head down and lurched forward. His shoulders jammed into Quinn's knees. Crying out in pain, Quinn tumbled on top of him. The two tangled on the ground, rolling in the dirt. Almost instantly Quinn took charge, straddling Corey as if he were a calf in a rodeo. He gripped Corey's neck, and in an instant Corey was gagging. "*Quinn . . . stop. . . .*"

"Isn't there anything you keep to yourself, Corey?" Quinn growled. "Do you understand what *private* means? Huh?"

"*You're—you're choking—cchchcghhhh!*" Corey said.

With a desperate burst of strength, Corey jammed the heel of his right hand into Quinn's jaw. He felt the grip loosen. With a cry of pain, Quinn let go, falling to the ground.

Corey slid away. He struggled to his feet, coughing like crazy. Quinn's hat had fallen off again, and Corey picked it up, flinging it at his attacker. "You think you have it so bad, poor thing," he snarled. "You want to know my secret? You want to know what I'm keeping private from you? Why I talk funny, and dress funny, and why I want to get back my stuff—and why what you just did was the stupidest thing in the history of the world?"

Quinn turned. His eyes were red, brimming with tears.

"I'm from the future, cowboy!" Corey blurted out. "Happy now? I was born in the twenty-first century, and that's the truth. Don't ask me how I got here. But without the artifacts I brought, I am stuck here with you. And it's the last place in the world I want to be."

Quinn stared at him, slack-jawed. "But that's . . ."

"Impossible?" Corey replied. "Yeah, I thought so, too, until it happened. And I don't care if you believe me or not."

Quinn shook his head. His eyes were wide and his skin seemed ashy. His mouth opened, but no words came out.

Corey stood, brushing himself off. He was sopping wet from head to foot and he felt miserable. "Must be nice getting away from those mean, naughty people in Wyoming. But at least you have someone to go home to."

He spun around and began walking back the way

he'd come. Anger and sadness and helplessness all collided in his brain. Quinn had been his friend. Having a friend had made all the difference. It had given Corey hope. Taken his mind away from the fact that he was stuck. A prisoner of time.

Now, as far as Corey was concerned, he might as well be dead.

But Quinn was right behind him. Corey felt a hand on his shoulder. "I have a secret, too," he murmured in a voice so soft Corey almost didn't hear it.

He turned. "What?"

"I said, I have a secret."

"I got that," Corey said. "I meant, 'What' as in 'What is the secret?'"

The cowboy stood, shaking out his hair. He let the rope fall to the ground. Without the ten-gallon hat, his head looked smaller than Corey had expected. "Quinn is a nickname," he said haltingly, "for Katherine."

28

Corey knew his reaction was wrong, but he couldn't help it. Somehow, the first thing that came out of his mouth was a big laugh.

Quinn's face fell. She was turning bright red. "I knew it. I should have kept my fat mouth shut."

"No! No!" Corey shouted. "I'm not laughing at you! Not at all. It's just that—well ... ."

"Well, what?" Quinn snapped.

"Well . . ." Corey shrugged. "So?"

"So?" Quinn looked baffled. "What do you mean?"

"I mean, so? You're cis female but you gender identify as male," Corey said. "Or is it not really a gender-fluidity thing, but just a disguise to get a job? Either way, what's the biggie?"

"Is that English?"

"The point is—why the big secret? What's wrong with you dressing and identifying as male?"

Quinn stared at him. Corey tried to read her expression but it seemed east of scared, west of baffled, north of furious, and south of relieved. "So . . . you don't think that's wrong?"

"Okay, okay, I think I get this—you're too out-there for 1917 Wyoming, right?" Corey's mind went through all the events of the last two days. "So, you and me sleeping on that bed . . . changing . . . going into the water with all those boys who had taken off their—"

"It wasn't proper," Quinn said.

Corey exhaled. He had to put his hand on his brow to keep his head from flying away. "Wow. That must have felt miserable, Quinn. Keeping that all bottled inside."

"I had no choice."

"Why? Why didn't you just tell me?"

"Because I didn't want you to think I was . . ." Quinn's voice trailed off, and she turned away.

"What?"

"*Abnormal*, okay?" Quinn said. "Perverted. Sinful. Bad."

"Wanting to be a boy is perverted?"

"Everyone but you thinks it is! I just wanted to get this job. I can do anything with horses a boy can do. The job advertisement was for boys and men only. So I dressed the part. I like boys' clothes, anyway. And my daddy was going to make me burn them and marry Buzz Hockenmeyer, which would have been a fate worse than death."

Corey took a deep breath. The sun was high, passing into afternoon, and the temperature was getting hot enough to dry them. Soon they would be just the way they had been. And then again, not.

He looked out toward the leafy, tranquil New Jersey shore across the river and imagined the steel-and-glass skyscrapers that were to come. "You know, a lot of things really suck in the twenty-first century," he said. "Trust me. But in some ways it's pretty cool. Well, *kids* are cool—some grown-ups maybe not so much. Anyway, if I could bring you back, you'd fit right in. You wouldn't have to hide or pretend." Corey smiled and put a gentle hand on Quinn's shoulder. "Don't think you're *bad*. Bad is torturing puppies or copying someone's homework or bullying or committing crimes. Bad is not what you are. You are normal. And you're right, you're better than the guys."

"Thanks, Corey." Quinn nodded, but Corey could

tell she didn't quite believe him. "I—I'm sorry I attacked you."

Corey rubbed his neck. "I'll survive."

"Say, if I help you find the thieves who took your stuff, will you take me to the future with you?"

"I can't, Quinn. I can't even get back myself. Besides, you'd hate it."

"You said I'd fit right in."

"But you'd have so much to adjust to. Nobody in the city rides horses. Cars are all over the place, and they go super fast. The skies are full of vehicles, too. They're called helicopters and jet planes. You can't swim in the river without getting diseases. People carry around their own telephones and spend the whole day looking at them."

"Well, if there are others like me, it would be worth it. There's nobody like me now."

"Yeah, there are," Corey replied. "You're in New York. You'll find them."

"Promise me when you go back, you'll look me up in your history books! 'Cause I plan to be famous."

"I'll google you."

Quinn glared at him. "I've shot at people for less."

"No! It's an internet—never mind," Corey said, feeling his face turn red. "Hey. Let's go back to the Better

Ridgefield. We'll take turns standing outside the door while the other takes a shower."

Quinn smiled. She looked quickly to either side. Then, as quick as a flick of her lasso, she leaned in and gave Corey a kiss. "Deal. Last one there is a rotten egg."

29

Leila didn't scream, and that was a big achievement. Auntie Flora, aka Catsquatch, had vanished along with her pile of possessions. Leila's bed and all her furniture were gone, too. Her bedroom was four blank walls. In the middle of the floor were stacks of cardboard boxes labeled GOTHAM MOVERS. Which meant that it was not yet her bedroom.

Because she had not been born yet.

"Ohhh-kay," Leila whispered to herself. "Hang on to your head, Leila."

The nail file, hot as an iron, fell from her hand. It tinkled as it hit the floor. During her whole life, Leila had never seen the wood floor beneath her carpet. The room was spotless, and poster-less, and she could smell the fresh paint. Outside the window, Central Park was a pattern of darkness and streetlamp lights. At least that looked the same.

No, not exactly. A rack of public bicycles, which had been installed on the sidewalk when she was little, was gone.

Leila had to steady herself against the wall. She wasn't prepared for this. When Auntie Flora told her to hold the nail file and try to mentally transport herself to 2001, she couldn't stop cracking up. That tiny nail file like some dollhouse Excalibur sword. It seemed ridiculous. She was sure Corey would be the only one who could do the real deed.

"Honey? Did you drop something?"

At the sound of her dad's voice, Leila choked back a gasp. He was here. Living here. Before Leila had even been born. Way before he had met the account executive with the small eyes and big feet and moved with her to Parsippany, New Jersey. Leila could not remember him ever calling her mom "honey." It was hard to imagine them ever being in love. It sounded so nice.

"I think something fell in the front room," came her mom's voice, sounding sweet and young.

At the thumping of footsteps, Leila scooped up the nail file and darted into the closet. Without all her stuff, it was empty and weirdly large. She shrank to the back wall, where one day there would be shelves.

Now Leila could hear the bedroom door open. She eyed the closet's doorknob. Beneath it was a keyhole. Carefully she kneeled down and looked through.

Mom was standing in the middle of the mess, gazing down at the floor. But not Mom exactly. It was as if one of Mom's old photos had come to life. Leila had seen her looking exactly like this, young and girlish, with the same floral shirt and high-waisted jeans. But here she was in three dimensions, breathing and walking and humming a tune Leila had never heard in her life.

She was dying to talk to her. What would happen if she just pushed the door open? Papou had explained that the past could not be changed, even if you tried. And her mom's past did not include meeting the thirteen-year-old Leila. If it had, Mom would have told her.

But maybe Leila was a Throwback, too. She'd made it this far. Mom might freak out a little, but she'd get it. She was a writer. She had an imagination. She was open-minded.

Leila put her hand on the doorknob and pushed the door open. But Mom was already out in the hallway, scurrying away. "Do you see the time, George?

We have a reservation at Ticker's!"

Ticker's. Columbus and Seventy-Fifth. Where they had met. When Leila was a little girl, there was a framed photo of them on the wall, standing happily in front of Ticker's. The place had gone out of business, right around the same time Mom and Dad's marriage had, too.

They were out of sight now, giggling and making kissy noises in the hallway. It gave Leila a funny, queasy feeling. She hung back in the room, listening as her parents rushed down the hallway and left the apartment.

She looked out her front window and waited a few moments. Her parents walked out the door, arm in arm. Dad had nearly a full head of brown hair, not yet gray and balding. Mom's was long, straight, and a deep brown that wasn't yet aided by a colorist.

They seemed so happy.

With a deep sigh, Leila sneaked out of the room. The hallway was bare and carpetless. All the photos that had gathered dust on the walls through her childhood hadn't yet been put up.

As she tiptoed past the kitchen, she glanced inside. The same old digital clock was on the wall, only without the chip from when Leila had dropped it at age nine.

It said 9:07 p.m., September 10, 2001.

She was here early. Corey had hopped to the morning of the eleventh, so he wouldn't be here yet. Leila heaved a sigh. She wanted to kick herself. If she'd waited till the morning, she wouldn't have to find someplace to hang for a whole night. She would have been able to get a full eight hours' sleep before traveling into the past.

For a brief moment she considered calling the creepy account executive with the small eyes and big feet from Parsippany and telling her to stay away from her dad.

Maybe another trip.

Now she had a job to do. Maybe she didn't need to wait until tomorrow morning.

She knew the odds of being a Throwback were slim.

But it wouldn't hurt to try.

30

Riding a horse was hard enough, but it was worse with a broomstick in your right hand and a seven-ton rope weighing your left shoulder down. "Do I have to carry this thing?" Corey grumbled.

"I got a great price—who'da thought? New York City?" Quinn said with a laugh. "You'll thank me for this when I teach you some roping. You need to know these skills. They'll come in handy someday."

"I'm sure," Corey grunted. As they rode from the horse shed to the train terminus, he was feeling pain in muscles he didn't know he possessed. Being a West Side cowboy was the last thing in the world he wanted to do.

At least he and Quinn had both caught a good long nap. During the day, the Better Ridgefield hadn't seemed so creepy. And Quinn was a lot less nervous now that she'd confided her big secret to Corey. "Hey, there she is—she's a beauty," Quinn said, gesturing toward a locomotive that faced north. She cupped her hand around her mouth and shouted, "*Well, howdy there, Mr. Conductor!*"

"Do you always have to be so cheerful?" Corey grumbled.

There were two men in the cab of the locomotive, a younger guy busily shoveling coal into a chute, and a silver-haired older guy with his hand on a lever. As Corey and Quinn approached the train, the older man leaned out his window on a deeply tanned elbow. His face was cragged and angular, his eyelids at half-mast, as if they had lost their will to stay open. He let loose a jet of brownish-black spit into a wooden bucket just a few feet from where Paisley now stood. The horse shied and backed away.

"Guess the old nag doesn't like surprises," the man said. He looked Corey and Quinn up and down and raised an eyebrow. "Well, well. Two of youse, huh?"

"We work well as a pair, sir," Quinn explained. "I

do the rope work, he clears with the precision lance. Complementary skills."

"If you're looking for compliments, this ain't the right place." *Chhhhppwwtt!* Another bull's-eye, right into the bucket. This guy was an Olympic-class spitter. "How old ya say you are?"

"Thirt—seventeen," Corey said.

"Eighteen," Quinn added.

"Yeah? So how come your voices ain't changed yet?" *Chhhhppwwtt!* "I know why. It's the food youse kids eat these days. Tell ya what I'll do—but only if you play yer cards right. Once we get past Gansevoort, I'll flip youse a little hunka somethin' that'll put hair on your chests. Maybe some pork loin. Or a slab of chuck."

"Thanks?" Corey said dubiously.

The guy's face twisted into a smile slowly, as if he wasn't used to doing it. "Don't let nobody say Mugsy Coleman ain't a genuous soul."

"What's 'playing our cards right'?" Quinn asked.

"Two words," Mugsy replied. "Clear. Them. Tracks. The last kid on the job, he got too confident, too far ahead. So some wino wanders on the track behind him and heads to the train like he wants to kiss it. I slam on the brakes. Now, we go pretty slow, but it takes a lot of time to stop this monster. I'll spare you the details, but suffice it to say, they have to cart the bum away in three bags. Plus I derail. Got me?"

"Got you," Corey replied. "But that was three words, not two."

"What?" Mugsy said.

"'Clear them tracks,'" Corey replied. "Three words. Another thing? It's either genuine or generous. There's no such word as *genuous*."

"'Zat so?"

Chhhhppwwtt!

That one landed outside the bucket, an inch from Paisley's hoof. The horse shied, jerking its neck back and nearly unseating Corey. Quinn reached out to steady Paisley's reins. "Don't be so smart," she whispered to Corey.

"Yer friend is making good sense," Mugsy said. "Time to work."

The train let out two small toots. Corey and Quinn both spurred their horses onward, heading uptown. For the first time, Corey looked upward into the skyline and really examined it. The city's profile was dense and low-slung. All the markers Corey was used to—the Empire State and Chrysler buildings, the glass towers along the river—were gone. The stone and brick buildings along Eleventh Avenue had orderly windowed surfaces like crossword puzzles, and in the setting sun those windows blazed fiery orange.

Corey rode to the right of the tracks, the city side. He tried to use a modified standing position, which eased the pain. Paisley liked to veer toward the buildings, but Corey kept pulling the reins. Riding Thunder, Quinn took the left side of the tracks, closer to the river. "Looking good, Corey," Quinn cried out. "You're a natural!"

"Th-th-thanks," Corey said through clenched teeth as he bounced in the saddle. "Can't wait to use . . . my precision lance. . . ."

Quinn laughed. "It sounded better than broom handle."

"I don't know . . . how long I can . . . do this. . . ."

"Think about that nice fat five dollars," Quinn said. "That oughtta get your energy back!"

"Where I come from . . . five bucks would get . . . an energy bar . . . ," Corey said.

Behind them, the train let out a horn blast so loud and deep that Corey could feel it in his spine. Paisley reared with a startled neigh. Letting go of the reins, Corey slid down the saddle.

With a yell, he landed in the dirt.

"Get back on!" Quinn screamed. "*Just get back on!*"

Corey scrambled to his feet, stepped into the stirrup, and nearly overshot the horse. As he settled into the saddle again, his heart was drumming. "I thought you said you could pick horses!"

"I can. I didn't know Paisley was like this." Quinn was looking over her shoulder, her face lined with disgust. "But I'll bet *they* knew, the bums."

Still shaking, Corey turned. Through the soot-stained window of the locomotive, he could see Mugsy Coleman and his assistant cracking up with laughter. "They did that on purpose?" Corey said. "That was a *joke?*"

"Next time," Quinn murmured, "let him say *genuous.*"

Corey chased away three chickens and a highly offended rooster. He poked away a tree branch and an empty bottle.

Quinn lassoed a garbage can, a broken chair, and an old, sleeping dog.

With every little success, Mugsy tooted the horn softly to celebrate. Paisley flinched each time, but Corey held tight.

"Hey, people in the future don't dump their trash

like this, do they?" Quinn asked.

"You don't want to know," Corey replied. He squinted at the track ahead. As the sun sank below the horizon, colors began to wash out to shades of gray. It was hard to tell shadows from real objects. Squirrels, rabbits, raccoons, and rats darted across the tracks in search of food.

"Feeding time for the critters," Quinn remarked as a fat old rabbit lumbered toward the river. "Ever had one of them?"

"*Had*, as in *tasted?*" Corey said. "No."

"Tastes just like chicken."

"Which is why we eat chicken and not bunny rabbits." Before the words could leave Corey's mouth, Quinn unhooked the rope from her shoulder and twirled it over her head. "Well, it's the wrong size rope for this, but I'm seeing some free supper!"

"No, Quinn," Corey said. "Don't—"

The rope hurtled through the air. It landed on the startled rabbit, who hopped straight upward in surprise. But the rope was a little thick for the body of a small animal. The rabbit slipped through and began hopping away, down the street toward the river.

Whooping and laughing, Quinn spurred Thunder

on and gave chase. They disappeared around a factory building en route to the waterfront. The train horn blasted again, and again Paisley shied. From behind him, Corey could hear Mugsy shouting angrily but couldn't make out the words.

Enough. This was not what Corey had bargained for. His body felt like it was going to split in two, his companion was off on a wild rabbit chase, and Mugsy was getting his kicks out of scaring a horse. This was not why he'd traveled into the past. None of this was getting him a step closer to going home.

"Quinn!" he shouted. *"Will you get back here—I can't do this alone!"*

As Paisley veered away from the track, Corey could hear the screech of the train's brakes. Mugsy's assistant was leaning out the window, his eyes bugged out, his arm pointing at something up the track.

"MAN AHEAD!"

This time Corey heard the words clearly. He spun in the saddle. To the right, about fifty yards ahead, a gate in the protective fence had been left open. A guy in gray baggy clothes was stumbling toward the tracks, past a tall cement shed. His toes jutted from his shoes, his hair was like a nest of loose wires, and he was having a lively conversation with a small bottle he held in his right hand.

Corey shouted at him, but he was too far away. As the man reached the track, his toes caught on the rail. He stared down for a moment, teetering. Then he dropped facedown into the path of the train.

31

Mugsy blasted the horn again, long and loud. Paisley recoiled, but Corey held tight.

In a split second, Corey's brain made a calculation. The train was massive. Its brakes were 1917 caliber. There was no way it would stop before making contact. But it was pretty far behind and going slow.

He gave Paisley a kick with both heels. *"Get him!"*

Paisley let out a snort, then quickly accelerated to a gallop. Corey clutched the reins. The fallen guy was lying on the track in a fetal position. His face was angled toward them, eyes shut tight. He was huge, at least two hundred pounds—too heavy and too unconscious to move with a broom handle.

As the horse pulled alongside the body, Corey

jumped off. Running to the man's side, he fell to his knees and grabbed his shoulders. *"Wake up!"*

Useless. The guy was dead weight.

"QUI-I-I-INNN!" Corey shouted, but his friend was behind the buildings that faced the river.

The train's brakes were screaming, and those screams were getting closer. Corey's nostrils filled with the sickly, acrid stink of burning metal. In his peripheral vision he saw the front of the locomotive looming slowly closer in a cloud of dust and smoke. He tried to pull the man away, but it was like lifting a hippo. The heavy rope fell from Corey's shoulder, landing on the guy's face, but even that didn't rouse him.

The rope.

Working as fast as he could, Corey lifted one end, tied it around the man's chest under his arms, and cinched the loop with a quick double knot. Pulling it tight, he held on to the other end of the rope, jumped to his feet, and ran to Paisley, who was shifting anxiously from hoof to hoof.

"Sorry about this, buddy," he said, wrapping his end of the rope tightly around Paisley's neck. "I think you're strong enough for this, right?"

Mounting the horse, he turned. The train was maybe twenty yards from the guy and gaining. Mugsy and his assistant were both staring at Corey as if he'd lost his mind. Corey pantomimed pulling an overhead rope. *"BLOW THE HORN!"* he shouted.

Mugsy got it right away and reached upward. The sound echoed off the walls of the buildings. Paisley whinnied and rose on his hind legs.

HO-O-O-O-ONNNNK!

"Go!" Corey shouted, kicking the horse's flank. "Run away! The train is coming for us!"

Paisley lunged forward. The rope went taut. The horse's body angled to the left with the added weight.

It took a few stuttering steps to build up speed. Corey's eyes were fixed on the track. The train was just a few feet away from the old guy and closing steadily. But his limp body was moving now, dragged by the rope, sliding over the rail and onto the gravel track bed. The head was clear . . . the shoulders . . .

A crowd had begun to form, mostly people in ragged clothes emerging from darkened doorways. A chorus of gasps and screams resounded, mixing with the continued screech of the train's brakes. Corey had to turn away. The clamor rose to a deafening pitch. A deep groan of shifting metal echoed against the buildings.

And then, a dull thump.

The horn, the brakes, and the cheers were all sucked away into an absence of sound. All Corey heard now was Paisley's hooves, clopping dutifully forward. He felt nauseated. He wasn't sure he wanted to see exactly what the horse was pulling. Or what it wasn't.

Gathering up his strength, Corey turned toward the track.

The first thing he saw was Mugsy's face in the window of the halted locomotive, ashen with shock.

Through a break in the crowd, Corey could see something on the ground. Something brown and wriggling.

"Gaaaahhhh! I apologize! Let me go! Sweet mother of life, let me go!"

Head, torso, two arms, two legs.

The man was there, all of him, fighting against the rope, trying to get loose. *"Whoa, Paisley, whoa!"* Corey shouted, pulling back on the reins.

The horse came to a halt. Corey jumped off and began running along the length of the rope. He pushed his way through the gawkers until he finally reached the bewildered old guy. The man was sitting up now, his cheeks bleeding and his eyes glassy. "What'd I do?" he cried.

Corey found the knot and quickly wrenched the

rope free. "I can't believe this worked. I—I don't know what I'm doing. You are so lucky."

"Worked? What happened to me?"

"You fell onto the tracks when the train was coming," Corey explained.

Through the locomotive window, Mugsy was shaking an angry fist and shouting. As the old man took in the scene, he murmured to himself and looked at Corey in amazement. "You—you're one of the cowboys," he said. "You saved me from . . . that?"

"I—I guess I did," Corey said.

The man wrapped his arms around Corey and began to sob. He reeked of alcohol and a body that probably hadn't showered in recent memory, but Corey didn't fight him. Laughter and "awwww"s sprang up around them. Corey felt people clapping his back. Someone began to applaud, and in a moment, the entire crowd joined in.

The man let go of Corey. His face was red, mottled, and teary, but he radiated gratitude. "Do I know you?" he said.

"No. I'm Corey Fletcher. From the Upper West Side."

"Oscar Schein. Bless you. Bless you, my boy!"

"Any time," Corey said.

"No offense, but I hope we never meet again," Oscar

said with a slow, impish smile. "At least not under these circumstances."

The old man broke into a wheezing laugh, and people in the crowd joined in. Corey felt bombarded by backslappers. Through the din he heard the clopping of hooves, and a familiar voice calling his name. Quinn was crossing the tracks on Thunder. Her face was bone white until she caught a glimpse of Corey. Jumping off the horse, she ran toward him. "Are you all right?"

"Yeah, he's all right," Oscar said. "He saved my life."

"I am so sorry I wasn't there!" Quinn said, her face lined with tears. "I—wait. You *lassoed* that guy?"

"It's a long story," Corey said with a laugh.

HO-O-O-O-ONNNNK! came the impatient sound of the train's horn.

"Mugsy thinks the story's already too long," Quinn said. "We'd better go. Give me the details later."

"Wait!" Oscar was moving his massive body, heaving himself to his feet. Eyeing Corey closely, he nodded. "Yeah, I do know you. You were the kid asleep in the Gash. The one Ratboy rolled."

"Someone named Ratboy took my stuff?" Corey said.

"What does he look like?" Quinn asked. "Besides a rat?"

"Nasty little guy, scrawny mustache, buckteeth, squeaks when he talks," Oscar replied. "Always bragging. Likes to steal from the trains and the barges. Most guys pawn their loot. This one's different. Cuts out the middleman and sells it himself. Makes a hundred, two hundred percent profit. Smarter than he looks, I think. Says he wants to set up a business buying and selling goods from overseas. Good luck with that, the lowlife. Anyways, I seen him in Grumney's just last night, on Washington and Bank. Tried to buy drinks for the house, but the bartender wouldn't take his money, told him it was fake."

"Wait. Why did he think it was fake?" Corey asked.

"All's I know," Oscar said, "is that Fritz the bartender, he keeps pointing to the bill and shouting 'Unmöglich!' Which is German for 'impossible.'"

Quinn and Corey exchanged a glance. Impossible could mean a lot of things. Like, the dates on the bills were from the future maybe. Which would make them seem counterfeit to a bartender in 1917. "Listen, I need to see this guy," Corey said.

"Ohhhh, you don't want to mix with Ratboy," Oscar replied. "'Cause the nickname don't just come from the way he looks but also from what's in his soul. I ain't got no trouble with him personally. But he eats his enemies, if you catch my drift."

Corey swallowed. "I'll take the risk."

"You're a kid."

"There are two of us," Corey pointed out.

"Well, you're crazy," Oscar said, "but he's at Grumney's every night at eleven on the dot. And there's an abandoned lot next door. I can get him in there, but then I leave him to you. And you better have a plan."

Quinn gave Corey a look. "You don't have to do this, you know. You can just stay here. It'll be fun. Exciting."

"You visiting from somewhere else?" Oscar asked. "I thought you said you were from the Upper West Side."

"I—" Corey didn't know what to say. Not to Oscar about time travel. Not to Quinn about the exact nature of the artifacts that would take him back.

He took a deep breath. Quinn's words echoed in his brain. *You can just stay here.* The idea was crazy. He couldn't take it seriously.

Still, she was cool, and he'd never met anyone like her. And for the teeniest fraction of a second, he thought it might not be the worst thing in the world.

HO-O-O-O-ONNNK! HO-O-O-O-ONNNK!

"*You guys having a tea party over there?*" Mugsy shouted. "*We're late on the pickup!*"

Corey grabbed Paisley's reins and looked at Quinn. "I need to go home," he said.

"This doesn't sound like a foolproof plan," Quinn remarked.

"Then I'll keep digging until I get one," Corey said.

Quinn sighed. "All right. But you'll miss me."

"Maybe I'll come back."

"I don't believe that for a minute," Quinn said. "But if you do, bring back some food."

"Woo-hoo," Corey said.

"Yee-hah." Corey stepped into the stirrup and mounted his horse. "See you at the lot near Grumney's at eleven o'clock, Mr. Schein!" he called out. "With Ratboy."

32

Leila used a tissue to scrub the mouthpiece of the clunky old telephone handset. It was gross looking—a round plastic thingy with a matrix of little holes that looked like they'd trapped germs, disease, and bad breath from thousands of New Yorkers since the beginning of time.

She could not fathom how people willingly used phone booths on the street to make calls. It wasn't as if they really needed to in 2001. Up and down Columbus Avenue near Ninety-Third, she could see a lot of people talking into cell phones. Yet just a few moments earlier, some old guy had grabbed the handset of the pay phone next to hers and grumbled, "You can't find a gosh darn phone booth anywhere these days!" Only he didn't actually say gosh darn.

But Leila wasn't picking up a signal on her own cell. Obviously iPhones weren't compatible with time travel. So it came to this. A phone booth.

Cradling the boat-shaped handset between her ear and shoulder, she read a sticker that had been smacked onto the huge box that contained the phone's buttons: For Information Dial 411.

She punched the number and waited. A mechanical voice prompt asked for a name. With an impatient sigh, Leila said, "Maria Fletcher."

"Marie O'Fincher," the voice responded. "If this is correct, press one. To try again, press two."

Leila pressed two. "MARIA . . ." She waited a moment. "FLETCH-ER."

"I am having trouble recognizing the name."

"Because you're a machine," Leila yelled. *"May I have a real person, please!"*

"Ariel Persson. If this is correct . . ."

"Aaaaagh!"

"I am having trouble recognizing the name."

About seven very frustrating minutes later, Leila had a phone number. She checked her watch. 10:31

p.m. Not too ridiculously late. Maria F. might be awake.

And if Leila could talk to her, maybe she could prevent her death.

This is crazy! a voice shouted in her head. The odds of Leila being a Throwback were teeny. Like, lottery odds. Maybe worse. Papou had failed to save Maria. Corey had failed to save her—and he *was* a Throwback.

Still.

She stared at the mouthpiece and took a deep breath. You never knew. Even if she could do nothing, she had nothing to lose.

Leila inserted two quarters into the phone and tapped out the number. After four rings, a male voice answered, "Hello?"

Leila choked back a gasp. She recognized the voice. It was a little more energetic, a little higher-pitched than she knew—younger, but unmistakably him. "Papou?" she said.

"Hello?" the voice repeated. "*Who* is it you're looking for?"

Leila cringed. Of course he didn't respond to the name *Papou*. He wasn't a grandfather yet.

But before she could reply, he blurted out, "Maria? Maria, is that you? Please, honey, talk to me. I miss you!"

"No, it's not. It's . . ." Leila's brain was spinning.

"It's a friend. Of Maria's. From college. Lily."

Lily? Leila almost hung up the phone right then, embarrassed by her own lameness.

"Oh, hi, Lily. She's not here. I'm her husband. We've . . . separated, I guess you'd call it. Temporarily."

Leila's jaw dropped. He'd actually fallen for it. "I'm so sorry! Um . . . are you still in touch? Is there a number where she can be reached?"

"I don't have the number at present. You know . . . we're working things out. You could leave a message at her work number. She'll get it first thing in the morning. Do you have a pen and paper?"

"Yes!" Leila lied.

As he gave her a number, Leila fumbled to pull a pen from her pants pocket. She scribbled the number on her arm while cradling the receiver between her ear and shoulder. "Thanks and, by the way," she said, "if you do talk to her, please tell her not to go to work tomorrow. I know it sounds nuts. But you have to believe me. I'm . . . like you. I can hop."

"Hop?"

"In time!" Leila said. "You know, like the Knickerbockers?"

"I'm afraid I don't know what you're talking about."

Leila cringed. He didn't know. In 2001, he must not

have started time traveling yet.

"So she's not to go to work," Papou continued. "And that would be because . . . ?"

"Because—because . . . ," Leila stammered. *Because a plane is going to fly into her building?* Anything she said would make her seem like a lunatic or a stalker. Still, she couldn't say *nothing*. "Because there is a report of a possible terrorist attack."

"Well, they tried that in ninety-three," Papou said wearily, "and they didn't get too far. Anyway, if you reach her first, please call me back and let me know."

"Will do."

She hung up, quickly inserted the coins into the pay phone, and tried the work number. She thought hard about what kind of message she would leave. The phone rang once . . . twice . . . three times.

Okay. Okay. Slow down, she told herself. It was silly to do this before planning out exactly what to say. As she pulled the phone away from her ear to hang up, she heard a voice that made her blood run cold.

"Karelian Group, Maria speaking."

33

Leila had taken first place in the Frederick Ruggles Middle School Improv Contest two years in a row, and she had captained the school debate team. She was known for thinking fast on her feet. But all she could manage over the phone was "Uh . . . you're at work?"

"Yes," said the voice of Corey's dead grandmother. She didn't sound at all like Leila expected. Not ghostly or saintly, not musical or magical. Just preoccupied and a little annoyed. "This is the Karelian Group, import-export. Who are you calling?"

"You!" Leila blurted. Her brain scrambled for some convincing excuse that would keep Maria F. on the phone. If Leila could do that, she might be able to set up a meeting. "We are . . . Nighttime Munchies! A . . . new food-delivery service for the World Trade Center area! Yeah. We specialize in fast, reliable delivery to hardworking New Yorkers at friendly prices."

Lame. Lame-o. World Series of Lameness.

She waited for an angry click at the other end. But instead she heard a muffled mumbling of voices, as if Corey's grandmother had placed her hand over the phone.

"Do you have pizza with pepperoni?" Maria finally asked.

"Sure!" Leila piped up. "I mean, we're a service, so we order from a number of restaurants and shops and bring the food to you! Just let us know if you have a favorite, and leave the rest to us!"

"Oh, okay. So . . . let's get this from Sal's on Church Street," Maria continued. "One large pepperoni; a pastrami sandwich on rye toast, extra mustard, no mayo; one turkey club, hold the bacon; one cheeseburger medium rare with fries; two Diet Cokes; three coffees; two bottles of seltzer; a brownie; two chocolate-chip cookies. Let me know if you need me to repeat it."

Leila was scribbling wildly all over the back of her

arm: *pizz pepp l—past rye xtr must no may*—1 *tclub no bac*—1 *cb med r* + *ff*—2 *DCs* 3 *cof* 2 *seltz—browny*—2 *chc chp cook.* "I got it all."

"Do you need my credit card info?" Maria asked.

"Yes!" Leila squeaked. She hadn't even thought of that. Her own cash would be too new, and her mom's credit card wouldn't work in the past. After taking down the info, she looked at her watch. She could call in the order from here, then twenty minutes for the cab ride downtown, another ten for the pickup and delivery . . . "That'll be half an hour to forty-five?"

"Half an hour would be better."

"On my way!"

Leila hung up the phone and shouted, "Yyyyyes!"

She darted to the curb, holding out her hand for a cab. She could google Sal's on the ride down and . . .

As a taxi screeched to a halt beside her, she realized the flaw in her logic. No cell reception. She didn't even know if Google existed. "Uh . . . never mind," she said to the driver. "Sorry."

She would need to get Sal's phone number first. The old-fashioned way. Running back to the pay phone, she lifted the receiver and tapped out 411 again. "The number for Sal's on Church Street?"

"Hello. You asked for Selsun Church. Is this correct?"

Leila hated 2001.

Getting through security at One World Trade Center was easy. The guy at the lobby desk took one look at her with the pizza box and all the bags from Sal's and waved her through. "Where you headed, miss? I'll let them know."

"Karelian?" Leila said.

"That'll be the ninety-fifth floor, last bank of elevators. You have a good night."

"Thanks! Hope you get to leave work and go home! Like, before tomorrow morning!"

The man smiled and bowed slightly. "Yes, I do. At midnight."

Leila felt a wash of relief. At least this guy would be alive and sleeping the next morning. His family would not be torn apart forever. He was lucky. But what about these other people?

All around, everyone else seemed placid, bored, content. A group of three bros exiting the elevator burst out laughing at some joke. Near the glass doors a couple stared dreamily into each other's eyes. A custodian pushed a broom, dancing to some music only she was hearing. How many of them would be here tomorrow morning? How was it fair that these people didn't know what was about to happen? How was it fair that she *could* know and they couldn't? Leila felt like everyone here was in some horrible recurring nightmare, a tragic Groundhog Day where you wake up over and over again on the day you die. Only she was the one who got to escape the dream.

Focus, she told herself. She had to focus.

As Leila headed across the polished floor, she could barely feel her feet touching the ground. She gulped panic-shortened breaths as she stepped into the elevator. Pressing 95, she closed her eyes and could not stop imagining herself rising through floors of black smoke, offices of dust.

At the ninety-fifth floor, the door slid open into a hallway facing a glass door. Beyond it was a vast office with sweeping views of the city and the two rivers. The carpet smelled new. Expensive-looking art had been carefully placed on the walls. As she approached a wall with a button marked After-Hour Deliveries, Press Here, Leila shook. Before she could touch it, a smiling young woman pushed open the door and said, "Yay!

Food! Hey, I'm Sarah. Come in, I'll show you to the conference room."

"Thanks." As Leila followed Sarah through the door and down another hallway, she felt herself starting to cry. Sarah wasn't much older than she was.

"Just leave it here and I'll get Maria. . . ." As Sarah opened the door to a big, empty room with a shiny oak desk, she turned to face Leila and her voice trailed off. "Hey, is everything all right?"

"Just . . . stay here when she comes in," Leila said. "Okay?"

Sarah looked at her uncertainly. "Um . . . okay."

She went away and returned in a moment with a woman who was tall and lanky like Corey, her hair a glorious mass of dark brown curls gathered in a haphazard ponytail. Her clothes were elegant and professional looking, and when she smiled Leila could see Corey behind her eyes. "Thanks very much," Maria said, reaching into a purse. "Let me give you a little something."

"I don't want a tip," Leila said, sitting. "I'm Leila. All I ask is a few minutes of your time. Sit?"

The two women exchanged a glance. Maria sat but Sarah remained standing by the door. "What is this all about?" Maria asked politely.

Leila took a deep breath and said, "I admit this is going to sound absolutely wack, but I know your grandson."

Maria laughed. "I don't have a grandson."

"I know. I know. You don't now," Leila said. "But your son and his wife will have a boy, and that boy will be named Corey. Corey Fletcher. They will live on West Ninety-Fifth Street."

"Oh?" Maria's eyes were darting toward the door.

"And I really, really want you to meet him someday."

"Well, I imagine I will," Maria said.

Leila shook her head. "He doesn't know you. He has never met you. If you listen to what I'm about to say, then he will. But I need your trust. You, too, Sarah. Because what I'm about to say will save your lives."

"I do trust you, Leila," Maria said, leaning forward on the table.

"You do?"

Maria nodded. "You seem like a sweet girl. Just tell me, how much did my husband pay you?"

Leila cocked her head. "Pay? Wait, you think Papou—I mean, you think your husband paid me to—"

"Get me to come back to him, yes. He's tried singing telegrams, flowers, and chocolates. He's been pestering our own children, and now they don't want to talk to either of us. He paid a mutual friend to fly all the way here from Oregon and talk me into returning to him. And now . . . soothsaying! Grandchildren!" She shook her head and gave a sad laugh. "I'm so sorry he's putting you through this."

"He's not putting me through anything!" Leila protested. "Look, there's this group of very special people. Here in New York they're called the Knickerbockers. Your husband will discover them after you—"

"After I what?"

"Die," Leila said.

Maria's tight smile vanished. "Excuse me?"

"I'm sorry. I know it sounds horrible. It is horrible. But let me explain. There are people who can travel in time. Your husband is one of them, and so am I. I can show you my school ID and my money, all dated from the future."

"I must ask you to go now." Maria stood. She pushed the food back to Leila. "And you can take this. I changed my mind about the order."

Leila sprang up from her seat. "You don't understand! You're going to die!"

Sarah was opening the glass door now. The security guard from downstairs lumbered through with another, bigger guard. They both looked baffled. "Did this girl threaten you, ma'am?"

"No," Maria said. "She just fooled me."

"Wait, *what*?" Leila said. "No! Please—"

"That's my fatal flaw, too," the guard said to Corey's grandmother with a sheepish smile. "I always trust a girl with pizza."

34

At 10:45 p.m. on Bank Street in 1917, there were more rats than people. Most of the gas lamps were shattered. The only two working ones cast small, pallid pools of light onto the cobblestones. At the end of the block, on Washington, an open door cast a third splotch of light. Raucous honky-tonk piano music and laughter blasted from within. "I'm guessing that's Grumney's," Corey whispered.

"Yup," Quinn whispered back.

"Do you see Oscar?" Corey continued whispering.

"No," Quinn said. "Do you?"

"No."

"So why are we whispering?"

"I don't know."

Quinn began walking in rhythm to the music, the clop of her cowboy boots echoing against the cobblestones. "Okay, let's repeat the plan," she said.

"Why?" Corey asked.

"Because I'm nervous," Quinn said. "And when I'm nervous, I forget things."

"Me, too." Corey took a deep breath. "Okay, so we know that Oscar knows this guy, Batboy."

"Ratboy."

"Right. We wait in the lot for Oscar to lure Ratboy in. You and I stick to the shadows. I distract him—"

"And then . . ." Quinn pantomimed whirling the lasso over her head. "We show him that crime does not pay!"

Corey nodded nervously. "Right. You rope him, and I get back all my stuff."

"Providing he has it," Quinn reminded him. "Which he might not. In which case, we say excuse me and run."

As they approached the end of the block, Corey could see an expanse of blackness the width of a brownstone, right next to the bar. "There's our empty lot," Quinn said.

It looked like once upon a time a wooden wall had been built across the lot to keep people out, but it was now a few cockeyed splintered panels like a gap-toothed grin. A rusted metal Keep Out sign lay on the ground, but it didn't seem necessary.

Beyond the wall was sheer blackness.

"We didn't bring a lantern," Corey groaned.

"Oops," Quinn said.

From behind the wall, Corey heard a shhhick sound, and a light flickered in the darkness. "That you, boys?" came a croaky voice.

Corey and Quinn stepped forward. "Oscar?" Corey said.

The light moved forward, through one of the panels. It revealed the face of Oscar Schein, who was holding out a kerosene lamp. Lit from below, his fleshy, friendly face seemed almost sinister, the crags deep and shadowy. "Bless you, boys," he said. "I been crying all night. With gratitude for my good fortune. From this day on, Oscar Schein turns over a new leaf, you mark my words! I got no use for these lowlifes and sinful honky-tonks no more. Tonight, for you, I deliver Ratboy."

"Have you seen him?" Corey asked.

"Not yet, but don't worry." Oscar looked up and down Bank Street. "For a corrupt, evil butcher of men, he's usually pretty reliable."

"*Butcher of men?*" Corey repeated. "Seriously?"

Quinn gulped. "What if you're younger than men?"

"Aaah, we ain't afraid, are we?" Oscar lifted a sharp, jagged stone from the ground. "One solid smack on the back of his rodent head with this, and it's lights out! Hee-hee!"

"Um, that's a great plan, but we thought of one that might not involve homicide," Corey said. "All you have to do is lure him into the darkness, Oscar. Quinn and I will take care of the rest."

A distant sound of whistling made Corey whirl around. His eyes widened at the sight of a silhouette approaching two blocks away.

Oscar dropped the rock and began waddling back into the black lot. "Have it your way, fellas. Come. Now."

Corey and Quinn scurried after him. The whistling grew louder. In the dim light of Oscar's lamp, the lot was a fluid moonscape of broken bottles, trash, branches, broken planks, scattered newspapers, and the swift movement of small animals. As Oscar flicked off the lantern, the area sank back into blackness. "You ready?" Oscar whispered.

Corey's eyes were adjusting to the dark. Enough light was entering from the door of Grumney's to outline the trash-strewn surface below. Corey looked at Quinn, who gave him a confident wink and a nod.

"Ready," Corey said.

As he and Quinn began walking deeper into the lot, Oscar began to count. "Five . . . four . . . three . . ."

The whistling was close now. It matched the tune from the piano inside Grumney's.

"Two . . . one . . ."

Corey felt his knees shaking. He turned to see Quinn unhooking the lasso from her shoulder.

"Now."

Oscar struck a match, lit his lamp, and stepped out onto the sidewalk. "We-e-e-ll, if it ain't my good friend Ratboy! What happened to your ugly face?"

"Scheino the wino!" came a hoarse, growly voice. "I got cut up in a fight."

"What a surprise. Well, anything would be an improvement," Oscar said. "Say, I have a little something for you. Something that'll . . . shall we say, lift your spirits? Hee-hee! If your appointment book ain't too full, let me invite you into my humble chapeau!"

As Oscar turned and began walking into the lot, Corey and Quinn shrank back into the shadows.

"Ain't it humble *château?*" Ratboy grunted, following the old man. Corey couldn't see his features, but there was something familiar about the rail-thin body and the hunched posture.

"What say?" Oscar replied.

"Château," Ratboy said. "That means 'house.' Chapeau is 'hat.' You just invited me into your hat."

"Did I?" The two men were past the broken wall now. They were completely in the lot, hidden from the street, their footsteps crunching against the debris below. About halfway in, Oscar turned to Ratboy and held up the lamp. "I thought you came off the boat from Finland, old boy. When, pray tell, did you learn French?"

"I got me an education, fat man. I'm gonna be in business someday, buying and selling in some fancy skyscraper while you're passed out in your own piss."

Corey's breath caught in his throat. Of course the silhouette was familiar. He knew exactly who Ratboy was. He had last seen him lying in a pool of blood near the Gash.

"It's the plank guy," Corey murmured.

Ratboy's head snapped toward Corey. A bandage covered the entire right side of his face. "Who's that?"

"You're an ooga-ooga boy," Corey said. "The one Quinn knifed."

"Come into the light!" Ratboy demanded. He was stomping diagonally across the lot, his one good eye stretched wide open. "I recognize you. 'Smatter, your pal too chicken to face me? I can play his game." With his right hand, he reached into the belt of his pants and pulled out a knife of his own.

Out of the darkness came Quinn's voice: "*Round and round she goes, and where she stops . . .*"

Ratboy's movements were quick, jerky. He whirled around like a tap dancer as a lasso spun overhead, like the outline of a cloud. It dropped over his torso before he had a chance to jump away.

"*Everybody knows!*"

"What the—?" Quinn yanked the rope tight, and Ratboy slipped. He fell to the ground, banging his bandaged head on a discarded chair. "*Yeeeaaaghh!*"

"Oops, sorry about that," Quinn said.

Oscar stood over the skinny guy and let out a cackle. "So, tell me, fella, is *ooga-ooga* Finnish for

'Look at me, I'm a sucker'?"

"It's . . . English . . . for 'You're gonna die for this, old man'!" Ratboy jerked his body from side to side, sending a sharp kick upward to Oscar's underside.

Oscar staggered away with a high-pitched scream. Ratboy somersaulted in Quinn's direction, the force of his movement yanking the lasso from Quinn's hands.

With a high-pitched yell like a trapped raccoon, Ratboy shook his body from side to side against the slackened rope, lifting his arms from the elbow. He raised the knife, angled it toward himself, and slid it under the rope. One good outward push sliced completely through the lasso, which flopped uselessly to the ground in pieces.

"Quinn, careful!" Corey shouted.

Ratboy's half face broke into a half grin. Spinning around, he pointed his knife into the darkness at Quinn. "You didn't take a big enough piece of me? You wanted to come back for more?"

"Wait, wait, time out, this is my fault, RB," Oscar said, lumbering toward Ratboy with a worried smile. "The kids don't mean you no harm. This is getting way out of hand. Stop it. Leave them alone. All they want to do is get back the money you took from the boy. Corey."

"I take money from a lot of—" Ratboy eyed Corey carefully. "Say, I know you. You're the kid with the weird-looking counterfeit bills, dated a hundred years in the future! You rotten chiseler. There I am, innocently using that cash to buy me a shirt, and you turn me into a criminal!"

Corey shook his head. "Wait. But if you stole them, you already were a crimin—"

"*Everybody's getting their jollies off old Ratboy, are they?*" Ratboy reached into his pocket with his free hand and pulled out a fistful of papers and small objects. "You want your useless junk? Here it is."

As he flung it outward, paper bills and coins scattered over the rocks and piles of trash. "*No-o-o-o!*" Corey screamed.

"Why so sad?" Ratboy hissed. "You can't take it where you're going. Hands in the air! All of you!"

Oscar and Corey obeyed, but Quinn stood with her hands on her hips defiantly, her back to the wall.

"Quinn!" Corey warned.

Yawning, Quinn raised her right hand.

"We'll do this one victim at a time," Ratboy said, raising his knife toward Quinn. "Eeny . . ."

He swung to Oscar. "Meeny . . ."

Then to Corey. "Miny . . ."

With a big grin, he crept toward Quinn, pulling back his knife arm.

"Moe."

35

Sometimes, Corey knew, thinking was overrated.

Like now.

Digging his feet into the rocks, he ran toward Ratboy and hurtled himself forward. He hit the skinny guy around the waist, knocking him off his feet. The two tumbled to the ground. Ratboy's knife flew away into the darkness. Corey heard it clank against a rock.

"Where did the shank go?" Oscar yelled.

Corey didn't have time to answer. He and Ratboy were rolling in the rubble. Corey felt a rock from below jab into his back, ripping through his shirt. He pushed the heel of his hand into Ratboy's bandage. As the man cried out in pain, Corey rolled him over and straddled him. Ratboy's white bandage had sprouted a deep red circle of blood that was growing larger. He reached for Corey's neck, but Corey swatted away his arms and dug his elbow into the guy's chest.

Ratboy groaned, breaking into a fit of coughing.

"I'll take care of him!" Quinn shouted, reaching down to grab Ratboy's shirt collar. "You find your artifact!"

As she brought the coughing ooga-ooga boy to his feet, Oscar handed the lantern to Corey. "I know how much you need your possessions, buddy boy. Take this, while I tidy up some personal business."

Oscar turned. With a windup like a retired minor-league pitcher, he landed a solid punch to Ratboy's good eye.

Quinn let out a whoop. "A shiner by Schein!"

Corey turned and dropped to his knees, lantern in hand. The floor of debris became a field of reflected light. He didn't care about the bills. All he needed was something metallic from the twenty-first century, a coin or the subway token. The lantern illuminated a galaxy of glinting—the quartz of broken stones, the edges of discarded metal utensils. Paper was everywhere, decaying piles of wrapped newspapers, discarded bags, magazines. Fallen branches and shattered wood reached skyward like begging arms. Corey could see a few dollar bills and a leather wallet, which must have belonged to Ratboy, or to someone Ratboy had robbed. The wallet felt like it had some coins in it so he stuffed it into his pocket. In the distance he saw the glint of Ratboy's knife. The hilt was jammed into the rocks, the point sticking at an angle into the air.

"Careful of that blade—it's near you!" he cried out. But he couldn't see the others. They'd disappeared into a dark corner, where he could hear scuffling and shouts. He rose to his feet and called out, "Everything okay? You guys need help?"

"Come join the fun!" Quinn replied.

As Corey ran forward, his foot caught on a thick old branch, wedged in the rocks. With a cry of pain, he dropped to his knees in a pile of rubble. His hand shot down instinctively.

About a foot beyond it, barely distinguishable in the dim light, was a thin yellow card with a black stripe. Corey froze. No one in 1917 would know what it was. No one in 1917 had ever seen a black magnetic strip. Or a New York City MetroCard.

His MetroCard. Which meant his other stuff must be nearby. Where this was, there had to be more. Something metallic.

Quickly he shoved the card into his shirt pocket.

He dug into the rocks and came up with handfuls of wrappers, dust, glass fragments, bits of fabric, shredded paper. Nothing at all from the stuff that was stolen, until he spotted the edge of his great-great-great-grandfather's passport. He dusted that off and pocketed it, too. Nice to have, but it wasn't going to help him. He found a quarter and a penny, but they were dated 1915 and 1916. They couldn't have been his. His coins must have fallen in different places. Or more likely, they were spent. Shopkeepers were less likely to look at the date of a coin than a bill.

As he shone the lantern over a wider area, he caught bits of color—magazine pages, a small New York Mets logo, a broken bit of a vase, a red ribbon. . . .

New York Mets. Corey crept closer, smiling. The Mets didn't exist until 1962.

And Mets-logo-themed cell phone cases didn't exist before cell phones.

"Got it . . . ," he said, barely above a whisper. He grabbed his iPhone off the ground and turned it over. The screen's plastic protective cover was scratched, but the screen was not cracked. Quickly he pressed the on/off button, and the startup logo began to glow. "*Quinn, I got it!*"

His answer was a loud scream.

Quinn's.

He jammed the phone into his pocket. Holding out the lantern, he ran toward the voices.

Quinn was crouched near the corner of the lot, breathing hard. Beside her, Oscar lay flat on the ground, groaning. "More . . . light . . ."

Corey swallowed hard. He knew he'd been away from them too long. Ratboy had taken advantage of the dark. He was a brawler, a gang member. He thrived off the darkness of New York City.

"Well, well, what is this?" Ratboy said, stepping into the light with a small leather book open in his hand. His bandage was completely red now, parts of it in tatters. With a grin, he began reading from the pages with his good eye: "'Dear Diary, First time writing since that odd night in the hotel. Shall I tell Corey today how I feel about him? He already knows my secret. Yes, Diary, it's true! And he doesn't care. He doesn't judge me or laugh at me or tell me I should wear a dress like a real girl or any of the things people tell me back home, and, oh, if I could only convince him to stay. . . .' Hoooooo-hooo-hahahaha! Oh, this'll be worth at least a couple of rounds of drinks at old Grumney's, while the boys mix tar and feathers for the midnight show!

Hahahaha, the tough old West Side cowboy is a sissy girl!"

"Give that back," Corey said, stepping toward him. He was seeing red. He hated every movement of every muscle on the man's face.

"Corey, don't," Quinn warned.

"*I said give that back!*" Ignoring Quinn's plea, he ran for Ratboy, swinging the lantern at his face.

With a giggle, Ratboy ducked easily out of the way. He dug his shoulders into Corey's abdomen, lifting him into the air and slamming him back down on the ground. With a quick swipe, Ratboy grabbed the lantern in one hand and scooped up the end of Quinn's lasso with the other.

Ratboy slammed the lantern against the brick wall, shattering the glass. The flames billowed outward, dancing freely in the night air. Holding the tip of the rope over the fire, he set it ablaze. "Plenty of kerosene in here," he taunted. "The better to anoint you all with, my dear. And, oh, what a flexible and flammable rope! The better to set you on fire! Who goes first? Old Oscar? Quinnie Two-Shoes?" He turned to Corey with a grin. "Or you, lover boy?"

"Me," Corey said.

Ratboy swung the lantern, and a spray of kerosene shot forward. Corey jumped back. "Run!" he called out.

Quinn stepped toward him, but she was stopped by the outstretched right arm of Oscar Schein. The big guy was struggling to his feet, eyeing Ratboy. His breathing was heavy, his face bright red.

As Ratboy pulled back the flaming lantern again, Oscar jumped. He dug his shoulder into the ooga-ooga boy's back. With a cry of surprise, Ratboy stumbled forward. He let go of the lantern and it crashed to the ground.

Ratboy lost his balance and dropped. Corey scrambled to his feet, the breath catching in his throat. Directly beneath the falling ooga-ooga boy, a triangle of metal glinted dully. It wasn't until the body made contact that Corey realized what it was.

The blade of Ratboy's own knife.

"No-o-o-o-o!" Corey cried out, as Ratboy landed on the blade with a sickening groan.

He lurched once and went still.

Corey flinched. As he turned to see his attacker's lifeless body, Oscar and Quinn ran to his side. "The blade . . . I knew it was there . . . ," Corey said. "I should have picked it up."

"Are you crazy, kid?" Oscar replied. "He was the

one who brought the knife here. He was going to use it on us. You didn't do nothing wrong."

The flaming rope lay on the ground beside Ratboy. As liquid began oozing out from underneath his body, Corey backed away. "Is that blood?"

"It's kerosene!" Quinn shouted. "Get away from here. Now!"

"But what about him?" Corey said. "What if he's alive?"

"We can't do anything for him now, kiddo," Oscar said. "Come on! This place is lousy with paper and old wood!"

The old man grabbed Corey by the wrist. As the three ran onto Bank Street, the lot began to glow like the dawn.

They ran past the bars and the alleyways. They crossed the dormant tracks and avoided the couples sneaking nighttime kisses against the buildings. They didn't stop until they reached the dock.

Quinn and Corey got there first. "You smell like kerosene," she said. "He got some on you. That was close, Corey. It could have been you."

She took a red bandanna from her pocket, shook it loose, and began blotting stains on Corey's shirt.

"Stop." Corey took the cloth from her, shoved it into his back pocket, and headed for the railing that over-looked the river. His brain was short-circuiting. "We were the ones who lured him into the lot, Quinn. He wasn't doing anything bad. And I—I—killed him."

"No," Quinn insisted. "That's not true. You didn't do a thing to him. He was coming for *you*. Corey, Rat-boy stole your possessions. Think about what he and his buddies tried to do to us at the Gash."

"I wasn't supposed to change history," Corey said. "That was a rule."

"You told me the whole point of this trip was to save your grandmother!" Quinn replied. "That's changing history."

"I was breaking the rule for *her*. But not for *this*. Coming to 1917 was an accident, Quinn. I never was supposed to be here. And now someone is dead who wouldn't have been."

Oscar was lumbering toward them now, short of breath. "That lowlife had it coming. You know how many people that gang has wiped out—or robbed, or tormented for their own fun? If he lives, more people will die. Besides, I'm the one that lured him in. If any-one's going to answer to the Almighty, it's me, Oscar Schein. And I'll be holding my head high, for the rest of my life and afterward. You gave that to me, Corey."

"And you, Oscar . . . ," Quinn said. "You gave Corey back his life."

Corey nodded. He was drained and sad, and not at all sure he should ever have tried to be a hero.

He was also ready, finally. He had the means to hop back. Nothing was stopping him now. "Thanks, guys," he said quietly. "I—I'll never forget you."

He looked at Quinn, but she glanced away, uptown toward the freight train depot a few blocks north. Her face was sunken and sad. "I guess I'll be going to work alone tomorrow."

Oscar looked curiously from Corey to Quinn. "The boy is leaving? Where's he headed?"

Quinn was in no mood to lie. "To the future, Oscar. Corey is a time traveler from the twenty-first century."

"Ah," Oscar said with a nod. "I thought he looked foreign. Didn't know you could do that sort of thing. But these days, with all the fancy new machines, pshew!" He gestured downtown, to where the Woolworth Building stood shiny and new, lit up by white lights and dwarfing every other building in the city. "If you can build something like that, you can do anything."

High above the white skyscraper, a shooting star

made its way through a thick spattering of white dots across the night sky. "You know," Corey said, "in the future you don't see stars like that in New York City."

"They blow 'em all up?" Oscar asked.

"Too much ambient light," Corey said. "The city will be full of cars capable of going seventy or eighty miles an hour, and lots of tall buildings."

"Well, nothing like that one, I imagine!" Oscar exclaimed. "It's the tallest in the world, by far."

"Three of them will surpass it, in about fifteen years," Corey said. "A few years later there'll be buildings of glass and steel, skyscrapers on every block in midtown and downtown, towers that rise and fall and are built again. These tracks? They'll be lifted off street level, into an elevated rail—and when there's no need for freight trains anymore, it becomes a park called the High Line. Everything in the city is lit—parks, offices, streets. Electricity runs the city. Light is everywhere. It's so bright it blocks the stars."

Oscar was staring at him, dumbfounded. "Who needs them, then? Where you're going, it sounds like you've got the stars in your hands."

Corey smiled. He looked at Quinn, but her eyes were rimmed with red. "I'll miss you."

Oscar put his arm on her shoulder. "Hey. Maybe he'll be back. I think he likes the stars. And some other very precious things."

The three of them turned to the river. A barge, close to the New Jersey shore, let out a low toot, moving slowly toward the Statue of Liberty. Corey closed his eyes, reached into his pocket, and held his cell phone.

He felt Quinn's arms around him. And he heard a soft whisper in his ear. "I'll always be with you."

"Me, too," Corey replied.

He closed his eyes. And he thought of home.

36

Corey's head was resting on a railroad tie. He sat bolt upright in a bed of gravel between tracks, surrounded by dried weeds and grasses. Quinn and Oscar were gone, but he heard a gasp behind him. When he spun around, his face was inches away from a pair of overalls.

"Whoa, where'd you come from, bro?" Above him loomed a guy in a baseball cap, leaning on a rake. "I coulda sworn nobody was here."

"What day is it?" Corey blurted.

"Your unlucky day," the guy said. "Because the High Line closes at ten, and I gotta kick you out. Your parents here, too?"

"No, it's just me." Standing, Corey glanced around.

Just ahead, a high-rise hotel straddled the tracks. A car horn sounded below him, along with bursts of laughter and pounding rap music. He was on the High Line trestle, above streets and shops and restaurants. Home. Glancing downtown, he saw no sign of the white Woolworth tower, although he knew it was there, hidden behind a dense thicket of glass skyscrapers.

Corey opened his hand. His phone was pinging notifications.

"Whoa. Dude. Look at you. Your shirt's all ripped. Your face is cut up. What happened?" the guard said, his brow creased with concern.

"It's a long story," Corey replied.

"I guess so. You just stay here a minute. Don't move." He turned and ran in the opposite direction, ducking into a shed tucked into the side of the High Line corridor. He came out with a folded blue work shirt and a big wad of moistened paper towels. "You're a big guy, this'll probably fit."

"Thanks," Corey said. As he took off his ripped shirt, the guy ran the wet paper towels down Corey's back. It stung, but it felt refreshing. The towel was red and mottled with pebbles when the guy pulled it away.

"Best I can do," the guy said. "None of my business, but I think you gotta get yourself home. Can I get you a cab? It'll be on me. As long as you don't live in, like, Pennsylvania."

Corey smiled. The shirt was way too baggy, but the fabric felt nice. "No thanks, I have my MetroCard. But that's really nice of you. I'll bring the shirt back."

"Gift of the New York City Parks Department." The guard smiled, and began leading him toward a locked gate. "Just don't let them know."

Corey nearly slept past the Ninety-Sixth Street station, but the conductor's voice woke him just in time. As he trudged up the steps to the sidewalk, a gust of autumn air blew in from Central Park across the street.

At the top of the stairs, he kept going straight. He knew the park would feel really good right then. Going home, waking everybody up, explaining what had happened and how he'd failed to save Maria—that wouldn't feel good.

The yellow taxis that barreled down Central Park West scared him. They looked like they were going ten times as fast as Corey remembered. The high-rises seemed ready to pounce. Even the trees seemed somehow too big. He'd only been away a short time, but the city had grown a hundred years older round him, and it would take a while for his brain to catch up.

He wondered what Quinn would say about all of this. It dawned on him that she could not possibly still be alive. And that made him feel a little wobbly.

He plopped down on a park bench, watching two dogs playfully roll around on the grass. His phone pinged again in his pocket, and he decided it was probably time to answer his messages. He couldn't pull the phone out, though, without extracting all the other junk inside—the passport, the old wallet, the bills. He set them down on the bench and scrolled through the list of messages. They were mostly from Mom, Dad, and Papou. He'd get back to them in a minute. They'd be glad he was safe and sound. But the message that caught his eye was the last one.

From Leila.

im back. where ru? pls pls pls pls answer!!!!!

With a deep breath, Corey answered her.

me too. my trip was a big FAIL. am in cp jst inside 96th. u?

He was pretty shocked when she answered in about a nanosecond.

dont move. am close by. b right there.

Corey texted her an okay, then looked at the text from Papou, sent an hour ago:

Hi! Visiting the house, believe it or not.
No one knows where you went.
Hurry back, we all want to see you!

Corey smiled. Papou had returned. Which meant he may have finally come clean to Mom and Dad. At least that was one secret Corey wouldn't have to keep.

He pocketed the phone again and reached for the pile on the park bench. The passport on top had fallen open. He lifted it and stared at the photo of his stoic-looking ancestor with the glaring eyes and walrus mustache. "Sorry we didn't meet, old Evanthis," he murmured. "You look like a super-fun guy."

Tucked under the passport was the thin leather wallet that Ratboy had thrown out along with his stuff. Corey figured it was something stolen from someone else. But when he picked it up, a carefully folded-up sheet of paper fell out. Corey unfolded it to see a photo of Ratboy's face staring out at him under the word Wanted. The first thing he noticed was that Ratboy's real first name was Eero. The second thing were the words "Thats me!!!" scribbled proudly atop the mug shot. Under the photo was a list of aliases. Aside from Ratboy, they included Finnin Haddie, the Swede, the Snake, the Blade, and Rod the Rodent.

"*Coreeeeeey!*" Corey did not spin around fast enough to avoid being attacked by a flying Leila. She leaped onto the bench, tackling him to the green wooden slats and sending the wallet and flyer onto the ground. "*You're aliiiiiive! I thought you were dead!*"

"So you're showing your joy by attacking me?" Corey said.

Leila sat up, letting him go. "I can do it, Corey. It's so crazy. I can hop like you. My aunt is a cat thing!"

"Slow down, Leila," Corey groaned. "My back is killing me and I had a really, really bad day."

"Okay. Okay." Leila took a deep breath. "Auntie Flora is one of those transspeciated people, or whatever you call it. Like Smig. It turns out she passed the time-travel gene to me, the way your *papou* passed it to you. That happens. It doesn't always go to sons and daughters. I didn't believe I could do it, Corey. But when you didn't come back, I thought you were in trouble. Or—or worse. So I had to try. Auntie Flora told me how to get to where you went—"

"Wait. Is this a joke? You went back to nine-eleven?"

"Look at me, Corey. This is not my joking face. I said I *tried*. But I went too early. I got there the night before."

"But you're not a Throwback, Leila!" Corey reminded her. "What did you think you were doing?"

"That's my point, Corey. What was I doing? I honestly don't know. When I got back, I felt like my brain had been put through a meat grinder. I kept trying to remember exactly what happened, but everything was mush. I know I was worried about you. I know I was thinking your mission wouldn't work, and if it didn't then maybe . . ." Leila turned away.

"You thought maybe I died," Corey said softly. "In the attack."

"Well . . . yeah. But what's wrong with me, Corey? Why can't I remember the details? Too traumatic?" Leila sighed and turned away. "That's what my shrink would say."

Corey shrugged. "I don't know. I wish I could forget too."

"Why?" Leila said. "What happened?"

Corey thought for a moment. How could he explain it all—the passport, the Gash, Horace Filcher and Haak's Pawnshop, ooga-ooga boys, the Better Ridgefield Hotel,

West Side cowboys, Oscar, Ratboy . . . and Quinn? How could he explain Quinn to anyone?

"Let's go to the house," Corey said. "Papou says he's there. I can tell you both at the same time." He scooped up the passport, the wallet, the flyer, and all the other random stuff that had fallen to the ground. Stuffing them into his pocket, he turned toward the exit.

"Corey?" Leila said, walking up beside him. "I have never seen you wear that shirt."

"Yeah. My shirt ripped. I got into a fight."

"And what's that in your back pocket?"

"I don't know." Corey stopped. His hand reached around back and felt a corner of cloth. He pulled it out and brought it around front.

It was a red bandanna that smelled of kerosene.

He smiled. Taking a deep breath, he shoved it back and began heading for the exit. "It's something a friend gave me."

37

It felt great to be home, but it felt horrible to have to tell Papou the truth. Corey shook as he and Leila walked down the stairs to the ground-floor apartment. Through the windows, he could see that the front living room was dark, and he had the sudden urge to run away.

Corey tried his apartment key, but it didn't fit. "Jammed," he said.

"You probably bent it," Leila said. "I do that all the time."

From behind them, a cat meowed. "Not now!" Leila hissed.

Corey turned to see an enormous white cat lumber away down the street. "Is that . . . ?"

"Auntie Flora, aka Catsquatch. We'll deal with her

later." Leila pressed her face to the window. "I think someone's in the kitchen."

Corey rapped gently but firmly on the door. When no one answered, he tried again. Just as he was reaching for the buzzer, the door swung open. An old-time movie star with a carefully groomed silver beard and a cashmere sweater beamed at them. "Heyyy, welcome! Long time no see, huh?"

Corey had to blink his eyes. "*Papou?*"

"I know, I look like I'm about a hundred years old, right? Come in, come in!" He ushered them both into the living room, turning on the overhead lights. "How about I throw in a log and start a fire, like the old days?"

"Papou, you . . . you . . ." Corey sank into a plush sofa facing a brick fireplace. Leila and he exchanged a baffled look as she sat stiffly next to him. Sunday *New York Times* magazines were stacked high on the coffee table, and all were open to the crossword puzzles. Every square was filled in with pen. "Wow, Papou, you clean up really nice. When did you get here?"

"Ha! Nicely! I clean up nicely," he declared, taking some kindling from a pile in a brass bucket. "Take care of your adverbs, *paithi mou*, and they will take care of you! Well, let's see, I guess we got here around noon.

Your mother was pretty galferstabbed, as you can imagine."

Leila cocked her head. "Galfer—?"

"Flabbergasted," Corey said. "He does anagrams on the spot."

"Bravo!" Papou said, beaming.

"Papou, you said *we*," Corey said. "'We got here around noon.' Who's we? You didn't bring Smig, did you?"

Papou put his finger to his lip. "Shhhh. But that's funny."

He had a big, expectant smile as he kneeled by the hearth. With quick, practiced movements, he threw in the kindling and rolled up some old newspapers among them. Then, after laying a log on top, he set the papers aflame. "There," he said, sitting back on an armchair. "So, Corey. Catch me up. I want every detail."

Corey swallowed hard. He realized that Papou knew. He had to know. And yet he was so upbeat, so excited about his own return to the family. "You're amazing, Papou. Really brave."

"I know," Papou replied with a laugh. "Tell me about you!"

"I'm—I'm sorry," Corey replied, fighting back the

urge to cry. "I'm so, so sorry. I tried. I really did. It just didn't work. But I can try again. I will. I promise. There's just one thing. I—I think I have to tell Mom and Dad. About the time traveling. Everybody has to know."

"Yes, of course," Papou said. "That was always part of the plan. Just as we said—"

"It's more than that. I had a scare, Papou. It was an accident. I went back a hundred years ago and almost got stuck in time."

Papou leaned forward. "Oh?"

"Corey?" Mrs. Fletcher was coming down the stairs now, dressed in a nightgown. "Where on earth have you been all day?"

Corey took a deep breath. He looked at his grandfather, who gave a nod. "I have a lot to say, Mom," Corey said. "But I need to say it with everybody here. The whole family."

His mother gave him a worried look. "All right," she said tentatively. "I'll go get Zenobia and your dad."

As she went upstairs, Papou stuck a poker in the fire and jostled the log. Sparks flew, rising upward. Corey's mind tumbled back a few hours, to a hundred years earlier. He thought about the small fires in the Gash. The coal furnace in the Tenth Avenue locomotive. The stars above the Hudson River. The flames that exploded from the top floors of the World Trade towers . . .

"Corey? Is that you?"

A voice called out behind him, a voice too strange to be heard in his own house, yet familiar in a way that made him feel light-headed and a little scared. He wasn't sure if it was real or part of his fever dream.

He turned.

Walking into the room was a woman with silver-black hair pulled into a ponytail, and that dream vanished like a spark into ash.

As Corey stumbled backward, falling on the sofa, she gave him a bright smile. "Guess what? We brought baklava, your favorite!"

He didn't know her.

But he knew exactly who she was.

He'd seen her on the corner of Washington and Liberty. He'd seen her look at him, frightened and fragile, her face thinner and her hair jet-black. He'd watched her run away from a good but confused husband, taking refuge in a thousand-foot-tall box that would turn her to dust.

"I—I couldn't stop you," he said, his mouth bone-dry. "You went back to work. . . ."

"You kicked me out of your office," Leila said.

Maria Fletcher sat on the arm of the sofa. Her smiling expression turned to confusion and she cast a quick glance to her husband.

"Are you okay, Corey?" Leila said. "You look like you just saw a ghost."

"Did you . . . *change* something?" Papou asked. "In the past?"

"No!" Corey shot back. "I wanted to. I tried to. Just like we planned it, on our walk from the park! You had just come back from Canada. You were homeless. You'd gone back four times to nine-eleven, to try to keep her from going to work in the tower!"

Papou got up from the chair and sat by Corey, taking him by the hand. His eyes were intense and urgent. "*Yiayia* and I live in Maine, Corey. I haven't been to Canada in years."

Corey was short of breath now. He turned to his grandmother. "And you . . . how did you escape?"

"I never worked in the World Trade Center, Corey," she said.

"No, you did!" Corey exclaimed. "Of course you did. At Karelian Group, in import-export!"

"Import-export, yes, but I've never heard of that firm," she said with a shrug, "and I've been in that business all my life, so I've heard of all of them. Our company's office was uptown."

Leila was tapping on her phone. "Corey . . . ," she said, her eyes fixed on the screen, "I'm looking at search results here. There is no Karelian Group. Does this have something to do with your time-hop?"

She didn't know.

Leila didn't know, and neither did Papou.

Their memories had adjusted to a new reality. A reality he had caused.

But how?

Corey's mouth felt like sandpaper. For a moment he said nothing, for fear his head might fly off. Now his whole family was coming down the stairs. If they were talking to him, asking him questions, he didn't hear them. Everything seemed to be going in slow motion.

He was picturing Ratboy's face but wasn't sure why.

Slowly he dug his hand into his pocket and fished out the wanted flyer. Shaking, he unfolded it and looked at the leering black-and-white photo of the man who had tried to kill him. The man who had died on his own knife, in a blaze set by the lantern he had smashed.

Corey ignored the list of aliases this time. Instead he focused on the label directly under his image.

His real name.

Eero Karelian.

I got me an education, fat man, he'd bragged to Oscar Schein. *I'm gonna be in business someday, buying and selling in some fancy skyscraper while you're passed out in your own piss.*

In the history of New York, Ratboy was destined to succeed. But you can't succeed if you're not alive.

The butterfly effect. One change leads to another. Frederick Ruggles's saved life. Ratboy Karelian's lost life.

The paper dropped to the floor and Corey looked up to his grandmother. His *yiayia.* "You wouldn't have wanted to work for them anyway," he said.

His grandmother gave him a curious smile. Mom, Dad, and Zenobia were staring at him, looking like they wanted to go back to sleep.

But his *papou's* eyes were tearing. Corey knew that somehow, he was figuring out what must have happened. "Oh dear God . . ." he murmured.

Corey would tell him all about it. Every detail. But that could wait.

He had a grandmother now, and it would be fun to get to know her.

He felt Leila's arm around his shoulder. He put his around her, too—and his other arm around Maria Harvoulakis Fletcher.

His own, honest-to-goodness *yiayia.*

She was looking at him with such love. She'd been

there. She'd seen him grow up. She knew him.

Would he ever gain those memories? Why hadn't his own mind "adjusted"?

There was so much he didn't understand. His thoughts flitted in his head like a small cave filled with a thousand bats.

He had to tell them. He had to explain what happened. But for now, he'd wait. The feeling was too good, and he wanted to savor it.

"I guess," he said, "we should have that baklava."

"We have baklava?" Zenobia shouted.

"Into the kitchen!" his dad announced.

Yiayia's smile was like starlight, her laugh like a song heard for the first time. She took Corey's hand and led him toward the kitchen. Her skin felt warm and soft and alive.

In his mind Corey heard a distant, Wyoming-accented voice shouting, "Yee-HAH!"

But he knew that was in his imagination. He had a big imagination.

Everyone said that.

And that was fine with him.

FOLLOW THE ADVENTURES OF

Jack McKinley in the mysterious, action-packed series that takes place throughout the Seven Wonders of the Ancient World.

For teaching guides, an interactive map, and videos, visit **www.sevenwondersbooks.com**

READ THE FURTHER ADVENTURES IN THE SEVEN WONDERS JOURNALS

More adventures by
PETER LERANGIS!